"Merry Christ

"Hello, Zoe," she heard a deep voice say on her cell phone.

Brent.

"Zoe...I called because I need your help."

"With what?" Putting up lights? A tree? Picking out presents? It was Christmas, so it could be anything. Maybe even an invitation to enjoy a hot cup of cocoa and friendly conversation by the fireplace inside that log cabin of his?

"Are you at home?" he asked.

Oh, this was definitely a moment to celebrate! "Yep."

"I have a problem," he continued. "A woman came by here earlier. She must've been confused about the location of the shelter and she left before I c—"

A baby's loud wail in the background cut sharply over the line, engulfing Brent's voice.

Oh, no. The warm feeling Brent's call had stirred in her froze to ice even as adrenaline pumped through her veins. "I'm on my way."

April Arrington grew up in a small town and developed a love for books at an early age. Emotionally moving stories have always held a special place in her heart. April enjoys collecting pottery and soaking up the Georgia sun on her front porch.

Books by April Arrington

Love Inspired

A Haven for His Twins
An Orphan's Holiday Home

Visit the Author Profile page at LoveInspired.com.

An Orphan's Holiday Home

APRIL ARRINGTON

LOVE INSPIRED

INSPIRATIONAL ROMANCE

LOVE INSPIRED®

INSPIRATIONAL ROMANCE

Recycling programs
for this product may
not exist in your area.

ISBN-13: 978-1-335-93680-6

An Orphan's Holiday Home

Copyright © 2024 by April Standard

Love Inspired
22 Adelaide St. West, 41st Floor
Toronto, Ontario M5H 4E3, Canada
www.LoveInspired.com

Printed in Lithuania

MIX
Paper | Supporting
responsible forestry
FSC® C021394

Thanks be unto God for his unspeakable gift.
—*2 Corinthians* 9:15

For those who see the pain of others this Christmas and give the gift of love.

Chapter One

Brent Carson preferred the dark. At midnight, the silence engulfing his log cabin seemed normal—after all, the sun was down, the moon was up and most people had slowed their busy steps, washed off the frustrations of the day and settled beneath the warm blankets on their beds.

Sitting in the dark, at a live-edge black-walnut desk in front of the picture window in his living room, Brent stared out at the winter stars shining brightly above Georgia's Blue Ridge Mountains and smiled as he pictured his wife, Kayla, sleeping peacefully upstairs in their bed, her long hair—as dark and sleek as a raven's wing—spread across his pillow, her pale hand resting against the warm mattress where his chest had been before he'd slipped out of bed and ventured downstairs. He pictured her stirring at his absence, her long lashes lifting, her bare feet touching the hardwood floor. He heard the stairs creaking softly beneath her quiet steps, smelled her light floral scent surrounding him, felt the press of her swollen belly against his back and her soft lips brush his cheek as she whispered, *We're cold. Come back to bed.*

Brent's smile died, the stars gradually disappeared and the sun rose.

This December morning, like every December morning for the past six years, began the same. When tendrils of sunlight reached the porch of the cabin, cascaded through the picture window and brightened the surface of the black-walnut desk, Brent retrieved a piece of blank stationery paper from a drawer and picked up his pen.

My dearest Kayla,
Today is December 1st...your favorite day of the year.

His smile returned.

Did you think I had forgotten? That I wouldn't remember your excitement each year? The way you'd grab my shoulders in bed and shake me hard until my eyes opened? The way you'd smile down at me, eager to start the day, and demand I get out of bed, put on my warmest coat and haul the axe out of the shed? The way you'd insist I follow you into the woods behind our home, saying that you knew where the perfect tree would be?

He closed his eyes and pictured their last December morning together, six years ago, when she'd led him out the back door of the log cabin and down the long dirt path that wound through the thick forest behind their home. She'd walked slower along the trail than she had in years prior, one warm hand curved protectively over her big, beautiful belly and the other clutching his, tugging him close as they'd ducked beneath low evergreen branches and woven their way deeper into the trees.

Our last Christmas tree was as perfect as you promised it would be. Seven feet tall, full branches and the greenest of greens...it filled the corner of our living room perfectly—almost as though it'd grown in place right through the hardwood floor.

A deep chuckle moved through his chest and escaped his lips as he recalled her standing in the living room beside it, smiling wide, rubbing her expectant belly with sparkling eyes as she'd said—

You said you didn't need any gifts under that tree. That I should save my money because you already had all you wanted: Us, together...and our baby girl—the best parts of us both—sleeping peacefully in your belly. A baby girl we would hold in our arms by Christmas Eve.

A chill swept over him, raising goose bumps on his neck and arms, and the odor of smoke drifted near as the warm fire he'd built in the fireplace hours earlier burned down to ash.

You promised it would be the best Christmas we'd ever had. You always kept your promises, and I know you would've kept this one, too, if God had allowed. And even then, when you stood beside that tree, if you'd known He would take you and our daughter from me, you wouldn't be angry—at least, not as angry as I still am—because you always believed God had a reason for everything.

I used to believe that, too.

His throat closed and he struggled to swallow, the words blurring before him on the page. His losses piled up, choking him, scorching his eyes and chest but leaving the rest of him frozen and numb.

People say I should've moved on by now, but I still miss you, Kayla. I wish—

He threw down the pen and rubbed his eyes, then, vision clear, folded the stationery paper into thirds and slid it into an envelope. Then he stood, carried it across the room and slid it inside a lone red stocking that hung from the fireplace mantel. He frowned at the German shepherd curled on the thick wool rug at his feet.

"Gettin' cold, Prince?"

The dog lifted his head and yawned, baring sharp white teeth, but his tongue lolled out of his mouth endearingly.

Brent removed his sherpa-lined denim jacket from the hook by the front door and shrugged it on. "Prince." He whistled, lifting his collar higher against his neck, then opened the front door. Cold winter air burst in, shooting another shiver through him. "Come on, boy. Take care of business while I grab some wood, all right?"

Prince blinked up at him lazily, then stood and headed toward the front door, pausing on the threshold to stretch, leaning in different directions to work each of his four legs individually and with great care.

Brent shivered again, his lips curving despite the chill. "Please, by all means, take your time. It's not like it's twenty degrees out there."

Prince lifted his nose at Brent and sniffed, then padded onto the front porch, paused for a neck stretch, then moseyed his way down the front steps, his long bushy tail swinging slowly behind him.

Brent managed a small smile. Prince had just turned

three last month and had already surpassed seventy pounds and reached twenty-five inches in height. Strong and healthy, Prince was an intimidating specimen to some, but Brent had learned early on that the German shepherd had a soft heart, and ever since the stray pup had shown up in his front yard on Christmas morning three years ago, Prince had been a consoling presence for Brent during his darkest days. Still was, if Brent were to be wholly honest with himself.

He followed Prince down the front steps then walked across the front lawn to the firewood shed and plundered through the stack for dry, seasoned logs. Prince sniffed the frost coating the latent brown grass, his nose seemingly catching an interesting scent, his long legs following the trail's direction.

"Take care of business, Prince." Brent stacked three logs in his arms, then grabbed another. "We're going back in soon."

Satisfied with the firewood he'd collected, Brent tipped his head back and surveyed the mountain range in the distance. Blues and pinks of different shades and intensities colored the mountaintops that formed his skyline as the rays of the sun glowed through, the low-hanging mist above the mountain peaks thin and fine, as though frozen in place. It was early season yet—the first dusting of snow wouldn't hit till mid-December, if then—but winter winds had already settled in, tugging the temperature down and casting an uncomfortable chill over the rugged landscape.

Prince barked, thrust his nose closer to the frosted ground and scoured the cold earth for the scent's source. He circled twice around the path leading to the dirt driveway, then back up to the cabin, halting at the foot of the steps, tail pointed and nose high in the air.

Brent frowned. "What is it, Prince?"

A raccoon, maybe? Opossum? Squirrel? With cooler temperatures and food growing scarce, it could be just about anything seeking warmth and com—

A sharp cry broke the still air.

Brent tilted his head. A rabbit? He'd heard one make that sound before. Could be a fox had gotten ahold of one? But wait…it wasn't exactly—

Another high-pitched wail. Prince barked, then sprang into action, bounding up the front steps, running across the porch and leaping up onto the wide, wooden porch swing with his two front paws. The wails continued, growing louder as Prince's barks joined them.

Cringing at the racket, Brent strode across the front lawn and ascended the porch, his steps slowing as he approached the wooden swing where Prince stood, his weight propped on his front paws. Beside his paws, a white basket shook, its walls shivering under the weight of movements from within.

"Prince." Heart pounding, Brent clutched the firewood he'd collected against his chest with one arm and grabbed the dog's collar with his free hand, tugging him back. "Get down."

Once Prince had backed away to a safe distance, Brent leaned in for a closer look. A pair of startled blue eyes stared back at him from above a soft pink blanket. Another sharp cry pierced the air as the small figure wiggled and a tiny, balled fist emerged, nudging the blanket aside, revealing the red, scrunched-up face of an infant in mid-cry.

"Oh no," Brent whispered. He stumbled backward, the

logs falling from his arms and slamming onto the porch floor, then visually scoured the expansive grounds of his property. There was a flash of movement through the evergreens. "Hey! You got the wrong house!"

A slight female figure with long red hair, clad in a white coat, disappeared into the thick tree line.

"Hey! Come back!" His voice turned hoarse, cold wind rattling his body. "The shelter's further down the mountain! I'm not who you're looking for!"

But he knew who the stranger expected would find the abandoned infant. Jessie Alden owned Hummingbird Haven, a shelter for abused women and abandoned children, just down the mountain. Only when he thought of who he could turn to for help with this situation, it wasn't Jessie's face that came to his mind.

Instead, Brent stood there, trembling in the winter wind, staring at the vulnerable, crying baby that had been abandoned on his porch, and thought of a woman with blond hair, green eyes and the brightest smile he'd ever seen. A woman who cared for others more than she did herself, who went out of her way to help and who had shown up at his door unannounced—and uninvited—more and more often over the past four years.

Zoe. She'd know exactly what to do.

Zoe Price loved lights. Every kind of light. Red, green, white, silver, gold, blue, lavender, orange, purple, hot pink...

Well, even she had to admit the hot pink might be a touch too much at Christmas. Or was it?

"How do you feel about the pink?" Zoe, standing in the living room of her small cabin at Hummingbird Haven, tilted her head and eyed the string of decorative lights draped across the fireplace mantel. She'd chosen the same shade for all of her Christmas décor this year. "Do you think it's garish?"

Miles, Zoe's five-year-old foster child, stilled in the act of unpacking a box of Christmas decorations and frowned. "What's *gar-ich* mean?"

"Garish," she corrected. "The pink lights might be garish. Repeat after me, please. *G-a-r-i-s-h.*"

Miles repeated the spelling as she'd taught him to do with all unfamiliar words. "*G-a-r-i-s-h.*"

"Garish means flashy," she said., "Kinda showy." She frowned, wrinkling her nose as she surveyed the lights again. "Too bright."

Miles shook his head. "No, ma'am. If you like them, I like them."

Zoe smiled, knelt beside him and tapped his nose. "I know what I like, but I'm asking what you like. Your opinion is important to me."

He stared up at her as he contemplated that for a few moments, his wide gaze roving over her face, uncertain and a bit skittish. "Um…then I like the lights." His teeth nibbled on his lower lip as he pointed over her shoulder, his expression hesitant. "But the socks are crooked."

Her heart squeezed, a strong sense of gratitude weaving through her as he summoned the courage to voice his opinion.

Months ago, Miles's mother—his only living relative—had packed her bags and left their apartment in the middle of the night, abandoning Miles and leaving him alone in an empty apartment. He'd waited two days for her return, and when she hadn't shown up or contacted him, Miles had gone to a neighbor for help. Soon after, he'd been placed at Hummingbird Haven. Jessie—Zoe's business partner and friend as well as owner of Hummingbird Haven—had noticed how quickly Zoe had taken to the boy and immediately agreed with Zoe when she'd suggested being Miles's foster parent.

Miles had barely spoken the first couple of weeks after he'd moved into Zoe's cabin, but over the past few months, with hours upon hours of support, dedication and love, Zoe, Jessie and Jessie's new husband, Holt, had managed to help him feel at ease enough to begin opening up to them all.

Still, sorrowful shadows haunted his dark eyes, and his mother's abandonment had left a seemingly indelible impact, instilling within him fears of making a mistake that might drive away another adult in his life and leave him alone—and feeling unloved—again.

"The socks?" Zoe glanced over her shoulder at the mantel where Miles pointed and smiled gently. The two hot-pink Christmas stockings—which had taken her forever to find in stores that only stocked green and red—matched the pink lights perfectly but were slightly askew. "Oh, yeah. I see what you mean, and we certainly can't have that. Christmas just wouldn't be the same with crooked stockings." She held out her arms. "Wanna give me a hand, mister?"

A hint of a grin lifted Miles's lips. Nodding, he turned around and backed into her arms, giggling as she lifted him on a deep groan.

"Oh, gracious!" She lifted Miles to her chest, arms wrapped around his middle and waddled over to the mantel, positioning him in front of one of the stockings. "What'd you eat for breakfast today? Bricks? Concrete?"

Miles giggled louder, the joyful sound warming Zoe's chest. "No! I didn't eat bricks!" His dark hair tickled her nose as he shook his head. "You made me pancakes and bacon and—"

"Syrup, oh my!" Zoe laughed and lifted him closer to the mantel. "Please straighten our stockings, my dear gentleman, so that we may have a proper Christmas."

Miles quaked in her arms with laughter as he straightened the pink Christmas stocking, tugging it to the left, right then center as she jiggled him around in her arms playfully. When he was satisfied with the position of the first stocking, she carried him, still waddling, along the mantel to the second stocking and laughed with him as he straightened that one, too.

Oh, it was so good to hear him giggle and see him smile!

"Is that good enough?" Miles asked, craning his neck to look back up at her, his smile widening.

Zoe nodded and lowered him gently to the floor. "You did perfect, sir."

Miles's brows rose. "You think Ms. Jessie and Mr. Holt will like it?"

"I think they'll love it," she said. "Especially the table decorations you put up in the community cabin. I can't wait to show them all your hard work when they get back. And tomorrow, it'll be time to put up the Santa mailbox."

Zoe rubbed her hands together, giddy with excitement. For the first time since they'd opened Hummingbird Haven together, Jessie had taken a vacation with her husband, Holt, and their newly adopted children to visit Holt's family for the Thanksgiving holidays. The new family had spent the past two weeks with Holt's relatives on their family farm in South Georgia. In the interim, Zoe had been given the go-ahead to decorate Hummingbird Haven's cabins. Tomorrow, she'd resume the annual tradition of putting up Santa's mailbox in Hope Springs's town square where Hope Springs residents, as well as those in neighboring mountain communities, could drop off a letter to Santa containing their wishes for this Christmas season.

The Santa mailbox was one of the festivities Zoe looked forward to the most each year. It was an incredible opportunity to share God's love with others…especially with those who may not know Him. Members of the church she attended partnered with local community leaders and business owners to raise funds, then divvy up, read and respond to the Dear Santa letters of local citizens with either a gift, a good deed or a heartfelt message. The activity was an opportunity for Zoe and other members of the community to do God's work and bring joy into the lives of others of all ages.

And most importantly this year, it would offer Zoe a chance to bring a hefty dose of cheer, goodwill and, hopefully, sense of love and belonging into Miles's life. He'd had such a difficult year and what she'd prayed for most of all so far this year was that she'd be able to help Miles feel loved, admired and at home. Though providing all of that for Miles successfully would require careful planning, organization and attention to detail.

Oh, boy. The first of December—Miles's first Christmas at Hummingbird Haven—and she was already behind schedule.

Zoe bit the nail on her pinky finger. "Actually, I was supposed to put up the mailbox yesterday, so it'd be good to go for receiving letters starting this morning, seeing as how today is the first day of December, but I underestimated how long it'd take us to decorate our cabin."

And she still wasn't done. Once she put up the Santa

mailbox tomorrow, she'd need to rake up the last of the fall leaves from the front driveway, finish stringing lights along the pathways between Hummingbird Haven's cabins, set up the nativity scene by the front entrance, cut down and put up a live tree in the community cabin. Then there was that beautiful outdoor scene of Santa kneeling in front of baby Jesus in a manger that she always placed by the Santa mailb—

Her cell phone vibrated in her jeans pocket. Still mentally listing the chores on her holiday to-do list, she tugged her cell phone out of her pocket and swiped the screen.

"Merry Christmas! You got Zoe."

"Zoe."

Brent. "Mercy."

Silence crossed the line, then the deep—somewhat grumpy—voice on the other end rumbled again. "What'd you say?"

Zoe nibbled harder on the nail of her pinky finger. Oh, gosh. He'd called. Brent Carson—the man she'd admired afar for years—had finally called. Although she'd given him her number over four years ago—one week after she'd first met him, but who was counting? And there was nothing wrong with being assertive, right?—he'd had yet to call…or seek her out even once.

Until today.

Today she hadn't had to go out of her way to casually bump into him in the hardware store and sneak a peek at those sad but gorgeous brown eyes or wander across the grocery store to the aisle where he was shopping to ask how he was doing and lean in to catch his soft voice, hoping he'd say more than two words to her. Today she hadn't had to stop by his cabin to buy five bottles of his homemade maple syrup—even though she had a dozen still in storage—and crack a corny joke just to see the corner of his downturned mouth lift with amusement for one point two milliseconds. And today she hadn't had to sneak a German shepherd pup onto his property as she had done one Christmas morning three years ago while she'd waited among frozen bushes, shivering in seventeen-degree weather, for him to find said pup and witness his one—and only!—full-blown, dazzling smile.

Today Brent Carson had finally called.

"Mercy," she repeated softly, her heart humming with a delight that had absolutely nothing to do with the gorgeous hot-pink lights she and Miles had just strung along the mantel and everything to do with the cheek-warming masculine voice on the other end of the line. "I said, mercy."

He fell silent again, then cleared his throat. "Zoe... I called because I need your help."

"With what?" Putting up lights? A tree? Picking out presents? It was Christmas, so it could be anything. Maybe asking for help was just an excuse and what he really wanted was to spend time with her. Maybe after a bit of Christmas help, they could enjoy a hot cup of cocoa and friendly conversation by the fireplace inside that cozy log cabin of his?

"Are you at home?" he asked.

Oh, this was definitely a moment to celebrate! "Yep."

"I have a problem," he continued. "A woman came by here earlier. She must've been confused about the location of the shelter, and she left before I c—"

A baby's loud wail in the background cut sharply over the line, engulfing Brent's voice.

Oh, no. The warm feeling Miles's laugh and Brent's call had stirred in her chest froze to ice even as adrenaline pumped through her veins. "I'm on my way."

Zoe ended the call, shoved the phone into her pocket and looked at Miles.

"Who was it?" he asked, blinking up at her.

She continued studying him—the tilt of his head, the concerned light in his eyes, the uncertain expression that appeared on his face. She tried to imagine how he'd felt the night his mother had left him. The confusion he must've felt, followed eventually by the realization, the fear…the pain. Then she tried to figure out how witnessing another child having been abandoned might potentially affect him now.

"It was Mr. Carson," she said. "He needs my help."

Zoe walked across the room to the window, staring out at the frost-tipped pines as their branches slowly thawed beneath the bright morning sun. Then she eyed the empty path leading from her cabin door through the trees toward Jessie's cabin.

Jessie and Holt wouldn't be home from Holt's family farm for hours. She'd have to see if one of the women staying in the other cabins might be available to watch Miles for a while. But it was Saturday—one of the only two days the residents had free from their new jobs each week—and the women at Hummingbird Haven—all of them abused—needed as much rest and stability as the children Hummingbird Haven sheltered. Not to mention, even if she could find a babysitter, Miles had barely left her side since he'd moved into her cabin at Hummingbird Haven and, apart from school, was reluctant to part from her.

Well, that was it, then. She'd have to take Miles with her.

Zoe returned to Miles and knelt beside him. "Someone left a baby with Mr. Carson that needs my help."

Miles examined her expression, then asked quietly, "Where's the baby's mom?"

She tucked one of his dark curls behind his ear gently, stalling. No matter how many children she'd rescued or taken in, witnessing the reality of child abandonment had never gotten easier. But it seemed all the more heartbreaking during the Christmas season. And one thing Miles, along with all the other children at Hummingbird Haven, needed was a sense of stability and security. Both of which required honesty.

"I think she's the one who left the baby," Zoe said.

Miles's chin trembled. "Forever? Like my mom left me?"

"I don't know." She cupped his cheek. "But I hope to find out."

"And you'll make sure the baby is safe?" he asked. "Like you did for me. 'Cause that's your job?"

She nodded. "Because I care. And because I believe it's what God would want me to do."

Miles stared up at her, then firmed his expression, the wobble in his chin subsiding. "Can I go, too?"

Zoe hesitated. "I'm afraid that may be the only choice we have, but when it comes to having guests at his home, Mr. Carson isn't always..."

Oh, how to put it? He wasn't always welcoming? Patient? Or...kind?

She'd hung up on Brent before she'd even thought to mention she may have to bring Miles with her. And Miles was still emotionally fragile and so eager for positive attention that one harsh or misguided word from Brent might—

"I care, too." Miles lifted his chin, voicing his first outspoken request for anything. "I want to go with you and help do what God wants you to do. And I want to see the baby. Please?"

Zoe looked at Miles, then glanced over her shoulder at the bright December morning. Perhaps knowing he wasn't alone in experiencing abandonment could be of help. Certainly any opportunity that might alleviate the misguided feelings of self-blame and guilt he still carried would be a blessing. And Zoe had learned years ago that helping others was always the best antidote to pain.

But no attempt she'd made over the years to help Brent overcome his great loss in life had worked. One thing she knew for certain was that Brent's pain was deep. So deep that, at times, he didn't stop to think of how capable he was of hurting others. And having a newborn abandoned at his home would have only added to his stress and grief.

Miles stared up at her, a pleading look in his wide eyes. "Please, Zoe?"

Zoe bit her thumbnail, trying to envision Brent's reaction to the unexpected presence of a second child in his home…and wondered if the affection she harbored for Brent would be enough to tame her temper if he did anything to hurt sweet Miles.

Chapter Two

Brent had no idea something so tiny could emit such an ear-splitting howl, and judging from the way Prince had curled into a ball in the corner of the living room, he imagined the past few minutes had been just as uncomfortable for the German shepherd as they had been for him.

"Please… I don't know what to do for you." Brent bent over the white basket he'd carried into his cabin earlier and set carefully on the soft leather sofa near the fireplace. "It's warm in here. I just put several logs on, see?" He motioned toward the crackling logs and bright flames licking high in the fireplace. "That's about as big a fire as you can build in that size of a firepl—"

The baby cried louder. Prince, still curled up on the rug by the fireplace, lowered his chin to the floor and covered his eyes with his paws.

"Okay, okay." Brent rubbed his temples as he studied the baby, beads of sweat breaking out on his forehead. "Obviously you're upset—with good reason…so what to try? Are you hungry or wet or something?"

More squalls. He looked down at his hands, stared at the rough skin, thick calluses and blunt fingertips which had never cradled an infant before—let alone one that was sobbing—then shoved them into his pockets.

"I'm not who you need. Your mom made a mistake, okay? She left you at the wrong h—"

He clamped his mouth shut, meeting the baby's wide, anguished eyes as he thought of the young woman he'd watched disappear into the woods just half an hour ago. How could she have done this? How could she have left a helpless infant on a stranger's porch in the cold and walked away without knowing for sure that she'd brought the child to the right place?

To make matters worse, he knew next to nothing about infants. Just the sound of the child crying before him provoked painful memories he still wrestled with on a daily basis and sent a piercing anguish through his gut that radiated throughout his extremities.

"Look…" Brent patted what looked to be a large diaper bag beside the basket on the sofa and tried again. "This bag was left with you, so maybe…uh…" He unzipped the bag and rifled through the contents with shaky hands. "Maybe there's, uh…"

Soft blankets, one rattle, two pairs of tiny wool socks, wipes and diapers—oh, no!

Nope. Not gonna happen. He wasn't equipped for changing a diaper. Besides, Zoe should be here any minute now. In fact, he had no idea why it was taking her so long. Seventeen minutes and—he glanced at his watch—twenty-seven seconds ago, she'd said she was on the way, and Hummingbird Haven was only a five-minute drive—at most—from his property. And the lungs on this baby… good night above! He considered himself fortunate not to have lost his hearing—and sanity—in that small span of time.

"Please, just calm down." Was that his voice? That high-pitched, desperate sound?

Prince, who'd been watching his every move with wide eyes, ducked his head and looked away.

Brent sucked in a deep breath and dug through the diaper bag some more. "Okay, I…uh, I think I found a—"

Jackpot!

"Here." His fingers fumbled, dropping a delicate pink-rimmed pacifier twice before withdrawing it from the bag, then he eased the pacifier close to the baby's mouth, touching the nipple to her lips. "Give this a try."

She tested it, then pushed it away with her tongue and thrashed her head, her cries increasing with an almost unbelievable intensity.

"Please try it?" Brent begged. Yep, he'd resorted to begging. "Please."

No go. This baby wasn't accepting his offering. Apparently whatever she needed, he didn't have.

Prince whimpered.

Just then, someone banged twice on the front door, and Brent almost sagged to his knees with relief as Prince sprang upright and barked at the sound of movement outside. Brent hustled across the room, nudging Prince back with one leg, and opened the door.

Zoe stood on his front porch, bundled in a puffy green jacket the same shade as her kind eyes, just as calm, poised and caring as he'd expected she would be in this situation. Prince, who'd always shown an abundance of affection whenever Zoe was present, shoved past Brent's leg and headbutted Zoe's middle.

"Hey, Prince. How are you, boy?" She bent, her wavy blond hair spilling over her shoulders as she wrapped her arms around Prince and hugged him gently while he licked her jean-clad leg. After a moment, she glanced up at

Brent beneath her thick lashes. "You have an unexpected visitor today, I take it?"

"Yeah." Wincing at the renewed cries emitting from farther inside his cabin, Brent swept an arm out toward his living room couch. "Thank you so much for coming. The baby's in here. I think there's something wrong with it. It hasn't stopped crying, and I wasn't sure if—"

"Miles, please wait right here with Mr. Carson." Zoe eased Prince aside, brushed past Brent and walked across his living room to the source of the cries, saying over her shoulder in a cautious tone, "Brent? You mind hanging out with Miles while I have a look-see?"

Brent looked down and found a young brown-haired boy, wrapped from head to toe in winter clothing, staring up at him, his small hand, snug in a thick blue glove, rubbing his red nose. Prince sniffed the boy's ankles, cast a sheepish look in the direction of the baby who still cried loudly in the living room, then lowered his head, ran down the porch steps and took refuge under the firewood shed.

The boy—Miles, was it?—still staring up at Brent, sniffed. "Cold air makes my nose run."

Brent stepped back.

The boy continued to stare. "Does it make your nose run, too, Mr. Carson?"

Brent shook his head, then, thinking better of it, nodded.

"You got a tissue in your pocket?" the boy asked, sniffing again. "Zoe always has one in hers, but I can't go ask her for it 'cause one of her ground rules says I gotta stay out here till she tells me I can come in."

Brent rubbed the back of his neck, where a tight knot was forming, and backed away more, then stilled mid-step, realizing something had changed.

The crying had stopped.

He glanced over his shoulder to where Zoe stood in his living room, cradling the baby, still bundled in a pink blanket, in her arms. She smoothed her palm over the infant's downy red head and whispered softly near the baby's ear, her pink lips curving into a bittersweet smile as she studied the baby's face.

"Is it okay?" Brent's voice sounded hoarse even to his own ears.

Zoe looked up, the bright flames of the fire glinting over a sheen of tears in her eyes. "*She* seems healthy and well, thanks to you bringing her in and warming her up."

Those green eyes and tender smile, coupled with the soft, calm breaths of the baby girl, protected and well, snuggled safe and comfortably in her arms...it was hard to look away. And even harder to keep his quaking legs steady beneath him as he thought of what should have been six years ago: Kayla and his own daughter, alive, safe and happy, together with him in this very room. Perhaps standing right there, cradling their baby girl, in the very same spot as Zoe.

Brent gritted his teeth and studied the vulnerable infant in Zoe's arms. As hard as it was to face his painful past, it was equally as difficult to peer into the baby's future, considering her early days had already been rife with such turmoil.

"What will happen to her now?" he asked.

Zoe returned her attention to the baby in her arms. "I need to take her to the hospital and have her medically cleared, then she'll come home with me and Miles to Hummingbird Haven for a while until more information is collected and additional decisions are made. But first I need to change her diaper." She dipped her chin toward the front right pocket of her jeans. "Do me a favor, please? Grab my cell and call the Baby Boarder Unit at Hope Springs Hospital. Sharon James is head nurse there, and she'll get us in right away."

Us? Brent held up his hands. "Look, I—"

"Front right pocket," she said. "Look for *Sharon J.* in my contacts. When she answers, I'll give you the information she'll ask you for."

"Can I come in now, Zoe?" Miles, still standing on the porch, shivered in the open doorway.

"Yes, you may," Zoe said, rocking the baby in her arms slowly and speaking in low, soothing tones. "Please close the door behind you to keep the draft out. Mr. Carson's built a cozy fire, and we don't want to dampen it."

Brent, surrounded by guests who he hadn't anticipated invading his personal space first thing on a Saturday morning, rubbed his sweaty palms across his jean-clad thighs. "Zoe, I think it's best if you just take her on to the hosp—"

"She won't be comfortable until I get this cold, wet diaper off, and the longer we discuss what to do, the longer it'll take to do it." She gave him a pointed look. "Front right pocket, please. Call *Sharon J.*"

He did as she asked, tugging her phone from her front pocket carefully with two fingers, finding Sharon's number on her phone and relaying information Zoe gave him when Sharon answered.

"And how long before Zoe arrives?" Sharon asked on the other end of the line.

"How long until you bring the baby to the hospital?" Brent relayed to Zoe, watching as she spread a quilt she'd pulled from the baby's bag over the sofa cushion.

"An hour, tops." Zoe gently settled the baby on the quilt, unwrapped the pink blanket swaddling her and grabbed a clean diaper from the bag. "Enough time to change her diaper, warm her back up and make the drive."

Brent relayed Zoe's answer to Sharon, thanked Sharon for her help, then disconnected the call. He studied the baby's face as Zoe changed her diaper, watching the infant's frightened eyes rove over the unfamiliar ceiling of his cabin, the fireplace, then settle on him. He couldn't imagine how afraid she must've been—abandoned by her mother and surrounded by strangers.

A tender ache unfurled in his chest. "Is…is there anything I can do to help?"

Zoe, having finished changing the baby's diaper, paused in tugging the baby's thick pink pants back on and glanced over her shoulder at Miles, who stood by the fireplace, wiping his nose with his gloved hand again. "Would you please give Miles a tissue?"

"Of course." Brent strode swiftly to the guest bathroom down the hall, pulled three soft tissues from a tissue dispenser on the sink, returned to the living room and offered the tissues to Miles.

"Thank you." Miles grabbed the tissues awkwardly with his gloved hand, pressed them to his nose and rubbed. "Arb blu gon to blosbital, too?"

Brent frowned. "I'm sorry—what?"

"He asked if you're going to the hospital, too." Zoe said, lifting the baby back into her arms.

Brent shook his head. "I'm afraid I wouldn't be of any use to you when it comes to a baby. I'd only be in the way."

Zoe cradled the infant, now warm, dry and heavy-eyed, closer to her chest and smiled. "If you say so. I can always call you and let you know how she's doing after Sharon gives her a check-up." She tilted her head. "I think you underestimate yourself, though. I'd say you were a lifesaver this morning. If you hadn't been here, she wouldn't have made it out there alone in the cold. It's a good thing you were home and not out, leading an impromptu excursion."

Brent glanced out the picture window, noting the cold mist had faded under the strong morning sun. Normally he'd either be on his boat, floating down the Toccoa River by now, leading a private fly-fishing excursion or on a steep mountain trail, guiding a small party of tourists on a day-long hike through the most scenic overlooks of the Blue Ridge Mountains. His business, Blue Ridge Excursions, which he'd started in his early twenties had grown steadily over the years…which was to be expected. After all, he had spent almost every day of each year out and about in the wilds of the mountains with strangers and every evening at his desk by the picture window, writing articles for tourist magazines to promote his business, except for one month out of each year: December.

He glanced at the lone stocking hanging on his mantel. In their early days of marriage, Kayla, who managed the schedule and financial matters of Blue Ridge Excursions, had steadfastly held to one request she'd reminded him of every year: that December belonged to their family. Brent had agreed and, whether a result of grief or just plain old nostalgia, he'd continued the tradition every year after Kayla's passing, closing his business on the last day of November and dedicating every day of December to Kayla's memory.

This year was no different.

"I still don't work in December," he said quietly. "Even though…"

His neck prickled, sensing the weight of Zoe's intense scrutiny.

"Anyway," he continued, "I get the feeling, somehow,

that the mom meant to stick around until someone found the baby. She was hiding in the woods and didn't take off until she saw me discover her daughter."

"What did she look like?" Zoe asked.

"Don't know. She took off so fast all I caught sight of was a redheaded female figure in a white coat." He frowned, remembering. "Though I did get the impression that she was young."

"It could've been anyone." Zoe smoothed her hand over the baby's red hair again. "This happens more often than you think. And she did the responsible thing—leaving her baby with someone rather than alone."

Brent sneaked a peek at Miles, who still stood by the fireplace, staring up intently at Kayla's stocking. From what he'd heard in town, the young boy's mother had abandoned him, too—except she'd left him on his own in an empty apartment. Miles had been blessed to end up at Hummingbird Haven and in Zoe's care—all the children living at the shelter were blessed. Zoe and Jessie worked hard to maintain a welcoming and supporting shelter that had earned its impressive reputation.

Brent's mouth twisted. So many couples in the world who hadn't been blessed with a baby of their own were desperate for a child to raise. For years, Kayla had dreamed of having a baby to love and cherish, and now this December, the same month Kayla would've given birth years ago if she'd survived labor, had arrived and there was finally a baby in his cabin but no mother to love it. And no Kayla.

Anger sparked in his gut—the same kind that reared its ugly head during his darkest moments of grief.

"Do you need anything else before you leave?" he forced past stiff lips.

Zoe's brows rose. "Well…would you mind taking the baby's bag to my Jeep? I can't carry both at one time, and it's cold out. That'll save me an extra trip back inside."

Grateful for the physical chore and an opportunity to hasten the baby's departure, he strode over to the couch, zipped up the baby's bag and carried it outside. He trudged across the cold ground to Zoe's Jeep, opened the door and tossed the bag into the back seat between a rear-facing car seat and a booster seat he assumed Miles used.

He stared at the car seat for just a moment, allowing his mind to briefly sift through painful memories of the day he and Kayla had bought a car seat of their own, then Kayla picking out a crib and him and Kayla assembling it in the nursery they'd prepared. Pregnancy had lent an endearingly clumsy air to Kayla and after dropping a tool several times, she'd settled into a rocking chair nearby and smiled, designating herself as supervisor as Brent, kissing her cheek and basking in her adoring gaze, had finished the work and imagined how their daughter would look bundled safely in the crib.

The smile that had risen to his lips at the memory fell. There had been so much love in both their hearts for their daughter—even months before she'd been born.

Brent's arms hung by his sides, heavy but empty. There was nothing he wouldn't give to hold his baby girl, to have her safe and protected in his arms right now. And he knew, without doubt, that Kayla would've done anything in her power to have had the chance to care for their baby…or the vulnerable one who'd been left at his door. But Kayla was no longer here—hadn't been for years—and when she had been alive, vibrant and full of joy, the decision hadn't been hers. It had belonged to God, and He'd chosen to take them both.

How cruel He could be.

Frown returning, Brent shut the Jeep's door and trudged back into his cabin, halting abruptly at the sight of Miles standing by the fireplace, holding Kayla's stocking.

"Put that back!"

Starting at the sharp crack of Brent's voice, the boy shoved one hand behind his back and the stocking fell from the other, hitting the floor. Miles's cheeks flushed. "I—I was o-only trying to f-fix it—"

"You shouldn't touch things that don't belong to you." Brent stalked across the room, snatched up the stocking and hung it back on the nail that protruded from the mantel.

"Brent." Zoe's calm tone broke through the fiery haze clouding his vision. "It wasn't his fault."

She stood, facing him, the baby still cradled against her chest with one arm while she held out the other, motioning for Miles to come to her. The boy did, slipping past Brent and burying his red face in her middle.

"It was my fault," she continued firmly. "The stocking was crooked, and Miles asked if he could straighten it. He helped me decorate my cabin for Christmas this morning, and he wanted to help you like he helped me. I gave him permission."

Wet heat filled Brent's eyes as he met her angry scrutiny. "That wasn't your place. You had no right."

She nodded, her tone softening. "I know, and I'm sorry. I was just trying to hel—"

"That's the problem." Venomous words sprang from his lips, searching for a target—any target within range—and he struggled, in vain, to stop them. "That's been the problem for years, ever since I met you. You show up at my door, uninvited and unannounced, buying maple syrup for the shelter that you could get for half the price at any store in town. You bump into me at the grocery store, the coffee shop and on the mountain trails. Supposedly you're always trying to check on me, trying to help. But what you're really doing is trying to pry into my life. Trying to intrude. Trying to change me." He shook his head. "That stocking doesn't belong to you. This isn't your cabin. And I'm not your—"

Her chin wobbled—just a bit. But that tiny falter in her ever-present calm, joyful disposition cut through him like a knife, collapsing the swell of anger within him and flooding him with a fresh wave of painful regret.

He'd known for years now—how could he not?—that Zoe had a soft spot for him. That she was attracted to him…as he was to her. An unwelcome situation, considering the fact that every time he allowed himself the briefest of moments to admire her bright smile, caring personality and kind eyes, he was overcome with guilt and memories of his vow to Kayla. So much so that each time Zoe approached him, he sought to escape her presence at the soonest opportunity—an act he'd known had hurt her more times than he cared to own up to.

But he suspected she wanted more than he'd be able to give. Perhaps more than he'd *want* to give to any woman ever again. And a woman as wonderful as her…well, she deserved a man who could love her with every secret corner of his heart.

"Go on," she said, her voice strained as she cradled the baby closer to her chest and tugged Miles closer to her side. "I'm not your what?"

He swallowed hard, his face flaming. "Zoe, I—"

"I'm not your friend? Neighbor? Someone who cares about your welfare?" Her words trembled. "I've tried to be all of those things," she said softly. "And maybe I shouldn't be since you don't want me to be. But today was different, don't you see? Today *you* were the one who called *me*."

He looked down and stared at his boots, blinked hard and tried to focus on the well-worn hem of his jeans that had begun to unravel.

"No matter how you feel about me," she said, "you have no right to take it out on Miles."

"Zoe—"

"Come on, Miles," she whispered. "Will you please help me get the baby in the car seat?"

Miles sniffed and blinked back a fresh surge of tears but nodded, his brown hair ruffling against Zoe's puffy jacket as he hugged her waist tight.

The three of them, Miles and Zoe holding the baby, moved past him, out the door and down the front porch steps. Prince ventured out from his hideout under the firewood shelter, trotted over to Zoe and butted her with his head, then licked Miles's wet, tear-stained cheeks and nuzzled the boy with his nose as she settled the baby in the car seat. Zoe knelt beside the German shepherd and hugged his neck, then helped Miles into the Jeep, climbed into the driver's seat and drove back down the steep driveway.

Brent squinted against the sunlight as it glinted off the windows of Zoe's white Jeep and watched her drive away. He continued standing there in the cold with Prince by his side, long after she'd gone, hot tears streaking down his own cheeks, feeling guiltier than ever.

Chapter Three

"I'll have a venti with three shots of espresso, four shots of cocoa, six pumps of peppermint syrup and eight sprays of whipped cream." Zoe, seated at the kitchen island in her cabin at Hummingbird Haven, slumped onto the butcher block countertop. "Oh, and one mini marshmallow, please."

Jessie, brewing fresh coffee on the other side of the kitchen, raised an eyebrow. "Just one?"

Zoe nodded. "I'm trying to watch my sugar intake."

Jessie's mouth quirked. "It's good to see Brent Carson didn't strip you of your sense of humor."

Mercy. Zoe clutched her chest. The mere mention of the man's name sent residual shockwaves of this morning's unfortunate encounter through her.

When Brent had called this morning asking for help, she'd been ecstatic that he'd reached out to her and eager to help both him and the infant left at his door. But Brent hadn't been as welcoming as she'd hoped, and nothing had turned out as she'd expected. Well…except for the only part of the morning that truly mattered: baby Holly—a name Zoe felt suited her new foster child—who, having been cleared by Sharon at the Boarder Baby Unit, now slept peacefully in a crib in Zoe's bedroom.

This morning's events had been scary at first—Zoe

was always terrified at what she might find when she received a call regarding an abandoned infant—but Holly had been deemed to be healthy, strong and, according to Sharon's estimate, about three weeks old. And despite the turmoil Holly had endured, she was now well fed, warm, dry and resting contentedly in a safe place with people who were eager to care for her.

Jessie, Zoe's business partner and best friend, had come through for Zoe as always, returning to Hummingbird Haven as soon as Zoe had texted, alerting her they had a new ward. Jessie had been waiting for Zoe at Zoe's cabin upon her return from the hospital and had stayed with Zoe ever since, setting up a crib in Zoe's bedroom, feeding Miles supper and helping him get ready for bed while Zoe had fed and soothed Holly, making her comfortable in her new home.

And now Jessie continued to stay, two hours after the sun had set, listening to Zoe air her grievances regarding Brent's outburst and providing a made-to-order Christmas coffee to soothe Zoe's strained nerves and crushed spirit.

"No," Zoe said, rubbing her fist against the ache in her chest and dredging up a small smile. "Brent didn't steal my sense of humor. I'm still filled to the brim with it. That and a whole lot of humility, heartbreak and degradation."

"And you think a cup of coffee diluted with an exorbitant amount of sugar will make you feel better?"

"Uh-uh. But it might keep me awake for the many times I'm sure Holly will wake during the night, needing to be fed and changed." Zoe narrowed her eyes, staring across the kitchen at the bright red coffee maker and one dozen glass jars, rims trimmed with holiday holly, stuffed with various cocoa and coffee condiments. "Do you know that Christmas coffee bar where you are, at this very moment, concocting my ridiculous beverage request is the one and only luxury I've afforded myself in four years? I bought it the same week I met Brent. I can still remember typing my credit card number on my laptop, choosing express delivery and dreaming of him standing right where you are, enjoying a delicious Christmas coffee with me and saying how glad he was that we met."

She couldn't have been more wrong.

Zoe smacked the countertop. "You know what? I'm not letting Brent steal my holiday joy! I'm going to use that Christmas coffee bar to make coffee twice a day, every day this month, and I'm going to enjoy draining every sugar-infused drop from every cup—whether I like it or not!"

"You know…" Jessie poured hot coffee into a massive Santa mug. "Brent isn't the only man walking the earth."

Zoe folded her arms on the counter and lowered her chin onto the back of her hands, the pain inside her running deeper than she cared to admit. "No. But I think I could've loved him. Maybe I already did a little, considering how badly his behavior hurt me today. From the moment I met him, I truly thought there was something meaningful between us. Was that naive of me, to think there may have been a future for us? To feel that strongly about someone who barely knows I exist?" She groaned. "I'm a grown woman. It's silly mooning over him like this, isn't it?"

"No," Jessie said softly. "In my opinion, some people don't acquaint themselves with their feelings enough. You've got a tender heart, Zoe, and you're optimistic. There's nothing wrong with that."

"He wouldn't even take a chance on getting to know me." Zoe stared at the wood grain of the countertop, the irregular patterns blurring before her. "Not even once."

Jessie remained silent for a minute, then said, "I know this is easy for me to say, but you'll get over him in time. Maybe even meet someone new who'll treat you like the treasure you are."

Zoe winced. "It's too hard to even think about meeting someone new right now." She sighed heavily, glancing at Jessie, who gathered ingredients at the coffee bar. "I already knew he wasn't really into me, but I thought I could at least be his friend or a helpful neighbor. Judging from his reaction this morning, I don't think he wants me to be either of those."

Steam curled above the rim of the jumbo Santa mug as Jessie doctored the coffee up with Zoe's sugar-infused additions. After the whipped-cream dispenser wheezed, signaling it was empty, Jessie tossed it into the trash, plopped one mini marshmallow on top of the melting white mound of whipped cream, then sat it on the counter in front of Zoe.

"Then love him as a Christian, and maybe, given time, the intensity of your romantic feelings for him will fade." Jessie smiled. "You've always been great at helping others feel God's love—especially at Christmas. Even if you might sometimes tend to…"

Zoe lifted her head long enough to sip a swallow of thick, syrupy coffee and lick the whipped cream from her lips. "To what?"

Jessie shrugged.

"Come on."

"It's nothing."

"Oh, come on, Jessie." Zoe shook her head. "I have no problem saying what's on my mind, and it won't hurt my feelings if you do the same."

Jessie lowered her head and avoided her gaze. "Brent hurt your feelings saying what was on his mind."

"That's different." Zoe strived for a nonchalant tone. "He's a man whose insults—and temper—I didn't ask for this morning. You're my best friend who I give permission to tell it to me like it is."

Jessie smiled. "That's what I admire most about you— you usually never let anything get you down for too long, and that's why I'm going to take you up on your offer and tell it to you like it is." Her chest lifted on a deep breath. "Sometimes—not all the time, mind you—but sometimes, in a very small way, you have a tendency to barge."

Zoe frowned. "Barge?"

"Barge," Jessie repeated. "Or in old-fashioned terms, you can, at times, be a barger."

"Seriously?" Zoe sat upright, her cheeks burning. "Me? A barger?"

"Only sometimes," Jessie confirmed. "And only with Brent, actually."

"Barger," a young voice piped from the kitchen doorway. Miles, clad in green pajamas littered with gleeful elves and holding something behind his back, furrowed his brow as he concentrated on spelling. "*B-a-r-j-u—*"

"Nope." Zoe shot to her feet, walked over to Miles and combed her fingers through his hair which was still damp from an evening shower. "There's no *j* or *u* in *barger*, Miles—just *g*'s and *e*'s—and just for the record, I'm not one." She kissed his cheek, then nudged him in the direction of the hallway. "Please go brush your teeth while I finish talking with Jessie, then I'll tuck you in."

"But—"

"I promise I won't be long, Miles." She returned to the kitchen island, took a hefty swig of coffee, then slumped against the counter again as she looked at Jessie. "Am I really a barger? You mean Brent was right about me?"

"No." Jessie said. "Absolutely not! You've tried to be a good neighbor—and friend—to Brent whether he chose to believe that or not. All I'm saying is we both know his outburst today arose from the fact that he's hurting, so maybe try coming at this from a different angle. Cheer him up in another way."

"A different angle?" Zoe knew she looked like an idiot, standing there, mouth gaping wide open, her mind a swirling black hole, but…what did Jessie mean, come at Brent from a different angle? "What other angle is there? Though quite frankly, I'm too hurt right now to even want to cheer him up. I've been dwelling on him so much I haven't even taken the time to put up my Christmas tree."

"What is it you always say?" Jessie asked. "'A person can be sad and still help others find joy.' And what's that other thing you're always saying? Oh, yeah. That the best antidote to pain is—"

"Helping others," Zoe grumbled. She crossed her arms over her chest. "But that's never worked when it came to Brent. I don't think he'd be very receptive to me attempting to help him again, seeing how rude he was to Miles and how he basically told me to kiss off this morning."

Kiss…and Brent in the same sentence. Oh, gracious, how her heart bled!

"But that's what I wanted to tell you." Miles, still standing on the threshold of the kitchen, moved his hands from behind his back and waved a folded piece of paper in the air. "Mr. Carson's sad, Zoe." He walked across the kitchen, stretched up onto the tips of his toes and waved the paper he held under Zoe's nose. "He's really sad. That's why he yelled at me."

The corner of the envelope clipped Zoe's chin. She made a face and took out the paper, unfolding it in her hands. "'My dearest Kayla,'" she read out loud. "Miles, what is this?"

"It's from the stocking," he whispered.

Frowning, Zoe glanced over her shoulder toward the living room at the pink stockings they'd hung on the mantel that morning. "Our stockings? I don't remember seeing this when we—"

"The stocking from Mr. Carson's house."

Zoe barely heard the words. Miles had shrunk away from her and stared down at his bare feet, his chin shoved tightly against his upper chest as he'd spoken.

Heart pounding, she knelt in front of him and tapped his chin, raising his face to hers. "Do you mean this letter belongs to Mr. Carson?"

Miles nodded, his eyes filling with tears. "Yes, but I didn't mean to take it. When I was trying to fix his stocking, it wouldn't go straight so I took it down and looked inside and saw the letter. That was what made it hang crooked."

Zoe blinked. "So you took the letter out of the stocking?"

He nodded again. "And I was gonna put it back—I promise I was—but Mr. Carson came in and yelled, and I got scared because what if he got mad at me for taking it out? So I put it in my pocket, and then I was too scared to try to give it back and I—"

"Took it with you." Groaning, Zoe sank back on her haunches and exchanged a worried look with Jessie. "So now it's here instead of there, where it should be."

Miles clutched her wrist with one hand and tapped the paper with the other. "It's sad, Zoe. I don't know all of the words—only some—but the ones I know sound sad."

Zoe groaned again. "You read it?" She opened her eyes and studied his face. He at least had the good grace to look suitably ashamed.

"Yes, ma'am."

"A letter that didn't belong to you," Zoe pointed out.

"Yes, ma'am." Miles sniffed as one big tear rolled down his flushed cheek. "I just wanted to see what it was. I thought it was Mr. Carson's letter to Santa, and I was gonna put it in the mailbox if it was. I'm sorry."

"Oh, Miles…" Zoe tugged him close and hugged him hard. At least he'd picked up the habit honestly, considering she herself was apparently a barger, too. "Boy, we've had a rough day, huh?"

He nodded, and his damp hair, smelling of baby shampoo and soap, tickled her nose.

"Thank you for being honest with me," she whispered. "But you'll have to take this letter back to Mr. Carson tomorrow afternoon and apologize."

He nodded again. "Yes, ma'am."

A low whimper and rustling sounded from a baby monitor on the kitchen island.

"Holly sounds a bit restless," Jessie said. "Why don't I tuck Miles in while I check on Holly and tell her goodbye for the night? It's about time I get going."

Zoe released Miles, wiped the tear from his chin and kissed his warm cheek. "Let Jessie tuck you in and get a good night's sleep, okay? We'll tackle this together tomorrow."

"Yes, ma'am." He hugged her neck, then said once more as Jessie lead him away, "I really am sorry, Zoe."

"I know. Good night, Miles."

She sat there, kneeling on the floor for several minutes, listening to Jessie check on baby Holly, then read a story softly to Miles in his bedroom down the hall, while staring at the letter in her hands.

Kayla. She must've been Brent's wife.

Zoe knew very little about Brent's past, but she knew his wife and child had died due to complications during childbirth several years ago. Jessie had told her that much…along with the fact that Brent, once outgoing and optimistic, had become a veritable recluse over the past six years, snapping and snarling at almost everyone he was forced to interact with outside of work—except for her. Whenever she ventured into his presence, he'd just stand there, his dark soulful eyes avoiding hers, and barely utter more than two words at a time.

That is until the awful scene in his cabin earlier this morning.

Brent's new reputation as a hard-nosed, no-nonsense outdoorsman had served him well in one aspect of his life at least: he never had a shortage of tourists for his excursions. They signed up in droves, wanting to experience the lesser-known waters and trails of the Blue Ridge Mountains with the grumpy guide who knew every inch of every mountain peak and added a fearless—almost brooding—atmosphere to his backwoods tours.

Brent was adventurous, Zoe admitted ruefully—there was no doubt about that—and the articles he wrote and sold to travel blogs and outdoorsy magazines revealed an almost tender appreciation for nature, both of which also contributed to his popularity. There was a constant line of tourists awaiting his tour services, eager to discover if the beauty of the Blue Ridge Mountains was as rich as it sounded in his articles.

Oh, great. There she went again, focusing on Brent's appealing traits instead of his faults. She'd do well to redirect her thoughts considering he'd made it abundantly clear this morning that he didn't share the same interest in her as she did in him. And on top of it all, she'd have to take Miles back to his cabin tomorrow and knock on his door, knowing they wouldn't be welcome.

Gracious! She'd have to barge into his presence again. The very act he'd complained about.

"Are you going to sit there all night?"

Zoe looked up, meeting Jessie's teasing gaze, and dredged up a small smile of her own. "I might. My legs are frozen. I thought about having to barge back into Brent's place tomorrow with Miles for an apology and became too despondent to move."

Jessie lifted one eyebrow, then reached down and grabbed Zoe's hands. "Get up, girl!" She pulled Zoe to her feet, spun her toward the kitchen and nudged her back onto a chair at the island. "Drink your sugar. Think good thoughts. Let God's grace take care of tomorrow's troubles."

Zoe stuck her mouth into the Santa mug, gathered a mouthful of what was left of the melting whipped cream and mumbled around it, "That's a lot easier to say than do."

"I know." Smiling, Jessie patted her back, then left, saying over her shoulder, "Get some rest while you can. I'll be by to help you get Holly ready for church in the morning."

Zoe stared across the empty kitchen, then down at the letter still clutched in her hands, her fingers itching to spread it out on the counter and get a closer look as Miles's words echoed in her mind.

Mr. Carson's sad, Zoe. He's really sad. That's why he yelled at me.

Slowly, she folded it back up and placed it on the counter, licked the last of the whipped cream from her lips and shook her head.

"I won't be a barger," she whispered. "I won't read it."

And she didn't. Until two hours, three cups of sugar-laden coffee and one baby's cry later.

Zoe sat on the same chair at the island, cradling baby Holly with one arm and feeding her a bottle with the other, her eyes glued to the letter she'd unfolded and spread out on the counter. She read the words scrawled to Kayla in Brent's heavy, masculine hand, tears pouring down her cheeks.

> *You promised it would be the best Christmas we'd ever had. You always kept your promises, and I know you would've kept this one, too, if God had allowed... you wouldn't be angry—at least, not as angry as I still am—because you always believed God had a reason for everything.*
>
> *I used to believe that, too.*

Zoe's breath caught, her heart breaking even more. Brent had lost so much. And no wonder he'd never returned her interest. He was still in love with his late wife—desperately so—and grief had taken hold of his soul.

And here she was, seated at her kitchen island, reading his private thoughts of anguish without his knowledge or permission.

"Oh, no," she whispered. "I *am* a barger."

Holly, sensing her discomfort, stopped suckling the bottle and blinked up at her with heavy-lidded eyes.

"Oh, it's okay, beautiful girl. I'm here for you." Zoe summoned a smile and studied Holly's face, noting the healthy bloom of pink in the baby's cheeks and the drowsy, contented expression. Her rosebud mouth curved just a bit, giving the impression of a fleeting smile.

Hours earlier, when Zoe had first heard Holly's anguished cries in Brent's cabin, she hadn't thought it would be possible to calm Holly, much less make her happy, but as always, she'd been willing to try. And now even the smallest of her efforts—a warm bath, dry diaper and full belly—seemed to be paying off. Holly had slept well for several hours after settling in the crib in her bedroom and after this feeding, she'd sleep peacefully for at least a couple hours more before her tummy would growl her awake again. And tomorrow Zoe would do everything in her power to make Holly happy every hour despite her broken heart.

Because she knew—as Jessie had reminded her—that the best antidote to pain was helping others.

You've always been great at helping others feel God's love—especially at Christmas.

Zoe propped Holly's bottle against the center of her chest and wiped her cheeks, picturing Brent alone at the large desk she'd noticed in his cabin that morning, writing to his late wife and growing angrier at God with every word.

"I can have a broken heart," she whispered to Holly, "and still help Brent find joy."

Zoe looked at the letter once more, then her eyes strayed from the kitchen to her living room where a thick decorative Christmas pillow on her sofa caught her attention. Her mind turned over ideas until one—the very best one—stuck. One that would hopefully brighten the season for Brent and make her less of a barger.

She kissed Holly's downy head and smiled, refusing to let it dim, even when what she prayed for hurt. "Lord, please help me bring Brent joy this Christmas. Then help me let him go."

Chapter Four

The first woman Brent had ever had reason to apologize to had been his mother. At sixteen years old, shortly after getting his driver's license, he'd driven himself and three friends to a house party one of his classmates had thrown. The night had been a fun one—so much so that he hadn't wanted it to end. So, he and his friends had stretched out the evening long past curfew, hanging out at the celebration until the cops had broken it up on account of a neighbor complaining about the noise, then relocated with a group of friends to a campsite to share laughs while exchanging admiring glances with the pretty girls sitting on the other side of a blazing bonfire.

It'd been dawn by the time he'd driven home, and his mother had met him at the door. She hadn't spoken—she hadn't needed to. The naked fear and distress in her tear-filled eyes as a result of his wordless absence had said it all. As had the surprise in her expression. For some reason, her silence at his behavior had cut him much deeper than any lecture of disappointment she could have delivered.

She'd been surprised that he—the well-behaved young gentleman she'd raised—would have behaved so carelessly at the first taste of freedom and caused her to fear for his safety and well-being in such a dismissive manner.

Hours later, he'd apologized and promised he'd never act in a way that would cause her to worry again. And he hadn't. The choices he'd made throughout his life from that point on, until his mother had passed away ten years ago, had been made only after careful consideration of how his actions would affect her.

He'd been teased for it. None of his friends—teenaged boys who thought of themselves as fully grown men— wanted to admit they kowtowed to their mothers' demands, but he'd been unashamed of his commitment and had never regretted it. The only regret he'd ever had on that score was breaking his mother's heart to begin with.

He harbored the same regret now, somewhere deep inside the center of his chest where a painful ache thrummed, as he stood on the porch of Zoe's cabin.

After his outburst yesterday afternoon, the last place he'd expected to put himself today was outside her door. But he owed her an apology—a heavy dose of guilt and sleepless night had been testament to that—and he'd found himself sitting at the desk in his cabin this morning and well into the afternoon, trying to envision Kayla, hear her voice and recall her touch, only for his hand to still over the stationery as his mind returned to the wounded expression on Zoe's face yesterday. He could still see her lips trembling with each callous word he'd thrown in her direction.

She definitely deserved an apology, and that ache in his chest grew more and more painful as each hour passed without him offering her one.

A bark echoed across the secluded landscape surrounding Zoe's cabin, emerging from beyond a thick line of trees at Brent's back.

He glanced over his shoulder and narrowed his eyes at a furious rustle of bushes nestled along the base of a metal pole supporting two bird feeders. Three cardinals and two crafty squirrels, who had been stuffing their bellies during the early hours of the cold afternoon, scattered in a flurry of fur and feathers.

"Prince!" Brent clapped. "Stop that." The pole shook, and the bird feeders swung precariously in different directions. "Leave the birds and squirrels alone."

The bushes stilled, and the bird feeders stopped swaying. Then a faint sneeze sounded, and the rustling resumed.

"Prince!" Brent patted his thigh. "Get over here."

He should've left the pup at home, but Prince, as usual, had clung to his heels as he'd left his cabin and walked to his truck, refusing to be ignored or left behind, and Brent couldn't, in good conscience, leave him closed up in the truck while he apologized to Zoe. Who knew how long he'd need to grovel to get back into her good graces?

But then again, letting Prince run rampant around Zoe's fragile bird feeders wasn't exactly ideal, either.

"Prin—"

"...not till we get..."

He stood up straighter at Zoe's muted voice on the other side of the closed door. No more time to worry about Prince—he needed to make sure he was presentable himself. He dragged a hand through his disheveled hair, tugged his denim jacket tighter around his chest, then knocked on the door.

"Just a sec!" Zoe's voice sounded again followed by a flurry of footsteps before the door opened. Her eyes met his, her mouth parting in surprise and her cheeks flushing a deep pink. "Oh."

She wore big elf ears and a fluffy pink stocking cap with bells and bows. On anyone else it might look silly, but on her it was cute. Endearing, even. Every bit as bright and playful as her disposition.

And he'd hurt her.

He dipped his head and attempted to smile, but the tight, uncomfortable set of his mouth told him he'd failed miserably. "Hi. I hope I didn't catch you at a bad time."

She stared at him, her mouth opening and closing silently, then she stepped back and shut the door in his face.

Oh, man. A heavy sigh billowed out of him. Clearly she was more upset than he'd imagined she might be. Maybe he should go home and try—

The door swung open again, startling him.

"No." She held up her pointer finger. "Not a bad time. Just hold on a sec, okay? Just…right there, yeah?"

Before he could answer, the door closed again.

There were frantic footsteps on the other side of the door, traveling from one side of the cabin to the other, what sounded like a couple of drawers opening and closing and the clink of what could've been dishes in the sink.

Brent capitalized on the delay, glancing over his shoulder at the bird feeders which rattled against the pole again. "Prince! Stop i—"

The door opened again. "Okay, I—"

Barks punctuated the still winter air, and Prince barreled out of the bushes, hot on a bushy-tailed red squirrel's trail, sending both bird feeders to the ground with a clang.

"Prince!" Brent smacked his thigh again. "Get over here!"

Prince continued barking and streaked faster across

the dormant grass of the front lawn, nipping at the furry tip of the squirrel's tail.

Zoe brought two fingers to her mouth and whistled. The sharp sound rattled Brent's eardrums but halted Prince in his tracks. Ears pointing, Prince looked at Zoe. His tongue lolled out, and he sprinted across the lawn, bounded up the steps and barreled headfirst into Zoe's legs.

"Oh, look at you, you big strong hunter." Zoe knelt on the porch and hugged Prince, murmuring sounds of praise as he licked her chin. "What did that sweet squirrel do to you, huh? Did he egg you on?"

Prince's bushy tail thumped frantically against the porch floor as he lapped more eagerly at her chin, practically bursting with delight at the praise.

Zoe laughed and lifted her chin out of reach. "He did, didn't he? That mean ol' teasing thing."

Brent's lip hitched as a bell on her pink stocking cap jangled, prompting Prince to leap upward and nip at it. "No, Prince." He grabbed Prince's collar and tugged the dog back to his side. "He likes noisy things."

Zoe stood, her face flushing. "Nosy things?"

"Noisy," he clarified.

The flush spread down her graceful neck, and her soft mouth tightened.

His skin prickled. "Not that you're noisy—or nosy. Just your hat, I mean."

He cringed, realizing how ridiculous his words sounded.

"But I am."

He stilled, then searched her expression. "You're what?"

"Noisy." She avoided his eyes. "And nosy."

He held up his hands. "No. I didn't mean that at al—"

"But it's true." She lifted her head then, met his gaze. "Unfortunately I'm both."

He sighed. "I didn't come by to argue again. As a matter of fact, I want to apologize to you and Miles—" he winced "—for the way I behaved yesterday. You came to help with the baby, and…well, instead of thanking you, I offended you and overreacted with Miles. I'd like to make it up to both of you."

She stared at him for a moment, then blinked and glanced over her shoulder, the bells on her stocking cap jangling again. "Miles?" she called out. "Mr. Carson is here. Would you come here for a minute? And bring what belongs to him, too, please."

Brent frowned. What could Miles or Zoe have that belonged to him?

Soft, hesitant footsteps approached the front door, then Miles emerged, huddling close behind Zoe, his brown eyes peeking around her waist and up at him. He wore the same type of stocking cap as Zoe, except his was green without bows, and he held a familiar envelope in his left hand. A small hand which trembled.

Brent's rib cage seemed to cave in, his breath leaving his constricted lungs in a painful whoosh.

"It's okay, Miles," Zoe said softly. "Go ahead."

Miles gulped, the small Adam's apple in his throat bobbing, as he lifted his hand and offered the envelope to Brent. "I-I took something that wasn't mine." His voice broke as he edged out from behind Zoe. "I… I'm sorry, Mr. Carson."

Brent took the envelope, nudged it open with his thumb and eyed the folded piece of stationery inside, his own hand shaking slightly.

"I found it when I was trying to fix your stocking and

was too afraid to put it back after you yelled." Miles lifted his trembling chin but managed to make eye contact. "But I should have. I should have given it back, and I shouldn't have read it. I'm sorry."

Brent stood there silently, the smooth envelope dangling between his fingertips as a cold wind swept hard at his back, cutting through his jacket and raising goose bumps on his arms even as a bead of sweat formed at his temple.

"Miles?" Zoe nudged the boy out onto the front porch. "Why don't you lead Prince around back and give him some water from the hose while Mr. Carson and I talk for a minute, okay?"

"Yes, ma'am." Miles darted around Brent, maintaining a wide berth, called out to Prince and ran down the front steps toward the back of the cabin. "Come on, Prince."

A heavy tug at Brent's right hand prompted Brent to release Prince's collar and allow the dog to dash off, galloping in Miles's wake.

"W-would you like to come in for a minute?" Zoe's hesitant voice cut through the stupor of his grief.

Brent turned away, stared at a squirrel darting across the front lawn in search of cover, then swallowed hard past the thick lump in his throat. "Okay."

When he faced her again, she was already walking back into her cabin, the bells on her festive hat jingling with each of her slow steps across the hardwood floor. He followed a few paces behind, the envelope in his hand shaking as a result of the tremors running through his arm.

"I, um…" Zoe stopped in front of a picture window by the front door and wove her fingers together as she looked up at him. "I'm so sorry, Brent. When I came to your cabin yesterday, I only meant to help—that's all. Truly. We just left so quickly and…" She cleared her throat. "We were already here when Miles told me he had your letter—"

"Did you read it, too?" He bit his lip to still the slight quiver in his chin.

She stilled, her wide green eyes holding his—captured almost—by his intense scrutiny. "Yes."

He exhaled, his chest tightening as he broke eye contact and walked, stiff legged, to the window. His eyes roamed the view blindly as he forced his mouth to move. "It was private."

"I know."

"Then why?"

"Because I'm a barger."

He turned his head to the side, straining to hear her whispered words.

"I'm always barging into your life," she continued. "Just like you said. And I have no excuse for it other than—than…"

He turned around and faced her head-on again. She visibly shrank away, her eyes skittering from his, her cheeks flushing. Her pale hands—usually so graceful and gentle—twisted together at her waist, her fingertips turning white.

"Do you think it was punishment?" He froze, shocked that the words had escaped his constricted throat and stiff lips.

She blinked up at him. "What?"

"Taking my wife and child from me?" His voice broke, but he ignored the nauseating churn in his gut and summoned a blank expression. "Do you think God did it to punish me?"

She looked dumbstruck, her mouth parting soundlessly.

"I've made mistakes." He grimaced. "Sinned. Maybe

I grew too distant from Him over the years. Maybe it's a lesson I needed to—"

"No." She shook her head, her long blond curls jostling against her shoulders. The bells jangling on her stocking cap. "I don't believe that." Her hands lifted toward him, then stopped in midair. Her chest lifted on a deep inhale as she shoved them into her pockets instead. "I believe God heals instead of hurts. But we live in an imperfect world where bad things happen, and I think death—" her shoulders lifted toward her ears "—is part of life."

The churn in his gut intensified as he tried to absorb her words, tried to accept them.

"I…" Zoe shook her head again, and her eyes sought his earnestly as she moved closer. "I'm so sorry you lost them. But you're a good man, Brent."

Was he? Brent looked down at her. He ached to lower his head, press his face against her warm neck, release the heavy sobs that clogged his throat and seek comfort in her embrace.

But a good man who loved his wife wouldn't do that, would he?

A plaintive cry and muffled movements punctured the silence between them.

Zoe moved away, picked up a baby monitor from the coffee table in the center of her living room and shrugged sheepishly. "Sorry. Holly's waking up from her nap."

He stared at the plastic object in her hand and tried to focus on her words instead of the ache of longing in his chest. "Holly?"

She smiled. "The baby. It's what Miles and I chose to name her on account of her red hair and it being Christmas." A self-conscious laugh burst from her lips. "Sounds silly, I suppose. But it seems to suit her."

"She's staying with you?"

Zoe nodded. "Until we know more. Jessie's working on trying to identify Holly's mom based on your description, but *red hair and a white coat* only gets her so far, you know? Of course, Holly's mom wanted anonymity, otherwise she wouldn't have brought Holly to Hummingbird Haven."

"To me, you mean?" Brent cringed at the memory of the baby crying on his front porch yesterday. "How is Holly?"

Zoe smiled. "She's doing great. She's too young to really understand or remember what's happened, and with a lot of comfort, nourishment and attention, she'll soon be thriving."

Relief spread through him. "I'm glad to hear that." He looked at the baby monitor again as Holly's whines grew louder, then turned toward the door. "I'll leave you to it, then."

"Wait."

He stopped at the urgent tone in Zoe's voice.

"We're, uh…" She touched the pink stocking cap on her head and smiled ruefully. "Miles and I don't dress like elves every day, you know? We planned on installing the Dear Santa mailbox in the town square this afternoon once Holly woke up from her nap." She looked down at her shoes. "Then we were going to swing by your place afterward, return your letter and apologize. And, well, we planned to invite you to participate in our Dear Santa letter project this Christmas." She raised her head, her smile returning, though it was still more tentative than usual. "But since you beat us to it, maybe you'd like to join us from the get-go and help install the mailbox, too?"

He frowned.

"Not like a...date-thing or whatever." She laughed, and her cheeks flushed a deeper shade of pink.

His frown—and confusion—deepened.

"What I mean," she said, "is that we put the Dear Santa mailbox up every year to help people who are in need and share God's love. We get letters from residents of all ages, and sometimes they're hurting." She nibbled on her lower lip as she searched his expression. "We write encouraging letters back to them, and for some, we perform good deeds—posing as Santa, of course. And we hope that by having Santa do God's work, those who don't know God's love will have an opportunity to feel cared for and maybe decide to get to know Him. The thing about it is that it lifts my spirit as much as I hope it does theirs. And I was thinking that maybe answering a few letters might help lift your spirits, too, you know?" She gestured toward the stationery in his hand and shifted awkwardly from one foot to the other. "Seeing as how you already write letters, maybe the change of topic might help you—"

"Forget?" He didn't mean to say the word so abruptly, with such animosity.

Zoe's smile dissipated. "No," she said softly. "I know you'll never forget Kayla or your baby girl." She spread her hands. "I just thought helping others might help brighten the season for you a little." Her tone lightened. "We only collect letters for a few weeks—through the holiday season—and you don't even have to do it that long. Maybe just try it for one week? And if you don't enjoy it, you can stop."

Brent rubbed the knot forming at the base of his neck and mulled it over. He supposed it wasn't asking too much. After all, he already wrote to Kayla regularly. Writing one more letter or two to comfort a stranger wouldn't be an inconvenience.

"You said you wanted to make it up to me and Miles," Zoe prompted. "If you help us install the mailbox and answer letters for one week, we'll be even. We've both apologized. I won't barge into your life anymore, and you will have made it up to me and Miles by doing a good deed. It's the Christian thing to do, and it's a win-win."

Considering the way he'd behaved, he guessed he owed it to her…and Miles. God, however…well, he didn't feel he owed God anything after what He'd taken from him.

Reluctantly, he nodded. "Okay. I'll give it a try."

Zoe's smile returned full blast. "Great!" She straightened her pink stocking cap, gave him a once-over, then tapped her chin thoughtfully. "There's just one more thing."

"What?"

She glanced at a thick decorative Christmas pillow resting on the sofa behind her, then looked pointedly at his middle as though sizing it up.

Heart racing, he covered his flat abs with both hands. "Oh, no. No way!"

One hour later, Zoe drove her Jeep, loaded with Santa's mailbox and Prince in the back, Miles and Holly in the back seat and Brent in the passenger seat, toward Hope Springs town square. So far, she'd managed to keep a straight face.

"Zoe?"

She glanced in the rearview mirror and surveyed Miles's anxious expression. "Hmm?"

"Isn't Santa supposed to have a big belly *and* be cheery?"

Zoe strove to maintain a neutral expression. "Yes."

Miles leaned forward and narrowed his eyes in Brent's direction. "He's got a big belly, but he ain't cheery."

"Isn't," Zoe corrected. "Not *ain't*."

She glanced at Brent, who glared at the curvy road winding ahead. It was hard to read the rest of his expression as the thick white beard hanging on his face obscured the lower half of his face. His belly though—made thick and round with the pillow from her sofa—strained against the black buttons on his bright red Santa suit, and he scratched his arms and chest vigorously, as he had done ever since he'd donned the Santa suit almost an hour ago.

"I don't think Mr. Carson is the right person to play Santa," Miles stated matter-of-factly.

Brent, yanking against the seat belt that snagged on his fake belly, swiveled in his seat to glare at Miles. "You think?"

That did it. Brent's grump of irritation cracked Zoe's composure, and she burst into laughter. "Don't worry, Miles. I think Mr. Carson—er, Santa's bark is worse than his bite."

Brent's gaze left Miles and fixated on Zoe's face, his angry scowl below the fuzzy white border of his festive Santa hat making her laugh harder.

Holly, sitting in her rear-facing car seat, released an uncomfortable-sounding whimper at the tense atmosphere in the Jeep's cab.

Miles frowned. "He looks kinda creepy, Zoe. And I think he's scaring Holly."

Zoe stopped laughing and struggled valiantly to regain a somber expression as she glanced at Brent. "Miles is right. Holly can't even see you but she still picked up on your grumpy vibe. Your scowl is a bit unsettling, Brent. You look like one of those murderous Santas in a late-night horror movie. You don't want to go around scaring babies today, do you?"

Brent sighed and faced forward again, smashing the pillow padding his middle below the seat belt. "No, I don't want to scare babies. But I don't want to wear this ridiculous outfit, either."

"I'm well aware of that." Zoe slowed the Jeep as Hope Springs's town square emerged into view. "But I told you how important it is that we maintain tradition, and Hope Springs's guidelines specify that volunteers aren't allowed to assist with the Santa mailbox unless they're in costume. I didn't have any more elf outfits—not that the ones I had would fit you—and it just so happened that the only Christmas costume left on hand at Hummingbird Haven was the Santa suit."

"I could've worn the reindeer headband," he mumbled, scratching his jaw beneath the fake beard.

"But then what would Prince have worn?" She glanced in the rearview mirror as Prince, having heard his name, popped his head up over the back seat. His tongue lolled. The antlers on his head were crooked, but he was absolutely adorable. "Those antlers were made for him."

Brent looked unconvinced. "You planned this, didn't you?"

Her neck heated. She tugged at the collar of her elf costume which suddenly felt uncomfortably tight.

"You did, didn't you?" Brent scoffed. "You thought about asking me to wear this Santa suit before I came by, didn't you?"

Zoe eased into one of the few empty parking spaces by the town square and sighed. "Yes, all right? The idea came to me last night after I read your let—" She tugged harder at her collar. "Let's just say I planned on bringing up the idea when Miles and I stopped by your place to apologize later this afternoon and discuss writing Dear Santa letters." She sat up straighter and flashed a smile. "But you came to us first and the opportunity presented itself, so I—"

"Took advantage."

"No." She met his dark eyes then, a stubborn gleam in her own. "I barged into your business one last time. I made a suggestion, which you accepted, remember? One week. A win-win, then we're even?"

He held her stare for a moment, then turned away and blew out a heavy breath that ruffled his fake beard. "Okay. Let's get this over with."

"Yay!" Zoe clapped her hands. "But Santa smiles, you know?"

He shot another glare in her direction and scratched the red material covering his armpit.

She shrugged. "I'm just saying. It wouldn't hurt you to crack a grin."

His mouth twitched, then his lips stretched into a vague semblance of a smile. Not a full-fledged cheery Santa smile but one decidedly less murderous.

"Excellent!" Zoe thrust her door open and waved her hand. "Come on. Let's get this party started, y'all."

She hopped out of the driver's seat and surveyed the scene before her as Brent and Miles exited the Jeep. Dozens of people milled about Hope Springs's town square: a group was busy unloading a twenty-foot-tall cypress tree that would serve as the town's Christmas tree, several people were unloading boxes of oversized Christmas decorations, five teenagers were untangling long strings of Christmas lights for the tree and a neat line of over a dozen people had formed near the tree.

"Where are we taking this thing?" Brent asked, opening the back door of the Jeep and patting the large old-fashioned mailbox in the back.

Zoe pointed at the line of people that had formed near the cypress tree. "Right there, where everyone's waiting. The Santa mailbox opens for business the same day and time every year in the town square." She puffed a strand of hair out of her face and straightened her pink stocking cap. "Unfortunately, I'm late. I should've had this up yesterday in preparation for today, but I had other business to attend to. And speaking of business—" she strode around the Jeep, opened the back passenger door and smiled down at Holly "—I'll bring our sweet Holly and Prince if you and Miles can handle the mailbox on your own?"

Miles, who stood beside Brent, peered up at Brent's floppy beard and protruding pillow belly, then shrugged at Zoe. "I guess."

It took several minutes and some effort to make it to the center of the town square with the mailbox, though that was to be expected considering she was dragging along one stubborn male. Prince, however, strained against his leash as Zoe led him across the sidewalk and latent grass toward the line of waiting people, eager to check out the new environment.

"They're here," a child at the front of the line shouted. "Santa and the elves are finally here!"

"And they brought a reindeer," a little girl yelled.

A collective gasp of awe rose from the children in the line.

"That's not a reindeer—that's a dog with antlers on," a boy shouted.

A groan of disappointment replaced the awe.

"I beg your pardon," Zoe said, smiling as she walked

past, cradling Holly to her chest and tugging her wrist against the leash handle looped around it to slow Prince down. "That is no ordinary dog. Prince happens to be Santa's best helper, and he's the one who led us here."

"Oh, yeah?" A boy, who looked to be around seven years old, propped his hands on his hips and curled his upper lip, flashing a missing front tooth. "Then where's his 'red nose, so bright'? How'd he lead you if he ain't got no red nose?"

"He doesn't have a red nose," Zoe corrected, "but he's bright where it counts." She tapped her temple. "Now, make way for Santa, please. He's brought what you've all been waiting for."

The line, made up of mostly children and parents, swayed to the side, each child tilting their head back to gape up at Brent as he carried the red mailbox past the line, then set it down, with Miles's help, on the lawn near the Christmas tree that had been raised and was now being decorated.

Brent straightened, scratched his lower back and armpit, then stared at the line of children gawking up at him.

"Well?" The boy missing a front tooth asked. "Ain't you gonna say nothing?"

"That's *aren't* you going to say anything." Zoe walked over to Brent's side and nudged him with her elbow. "And aren't you, Santa?" He looked at her blankly. "Going to say something, I mean?"

Brent stared back at her, a look akin to fear in his eyes. "This is a bad idea," he whispered, leaning in close. His warm breath tickled her cold earlobe. "Isn't it wrong to deceive these kids? And what about Miles? Me dressing up like this is bound to give him doubts about the big guy who comes down the chimney."

Zoe forced a bright smile for the line of children still gaping up at Brent and whispered back, "Miles understands you're standing in for the real Santa, so his excitement over Santa sliding down our chimney on Christmas Eve will remain intact. And please remember that Santa is here today to do God's work, so you need to be joyful, open and optimistic. These kids need to see some semblance of Santa in you, otherwise you might crush their sweet, fragile Christmas dreams."

Brent scowled. "Thanks for the pep talk."

"You're welcome," she whispered through her tight smile. "Now stop scowling and belt out a few *ho, ho, ho*s."

He squared his broad shoulders, cleared his throat, scratched at his baggy beard, then mumbled in an almost deadpan tone, "Ho, ho…ho."

The kids stared up at him silently. One of the dads who stood in the line snorted, and when his wife smacked his arm, he hid his laughter behind his hand.

Brent bristled. It seemed the athletic outdoorsman in him had a competitive streak that wouldn't allow him to fail because he raised one eyebrow at the laughing dad, put his shoulders back then, broad hands cupping his big belly, bellowed out a series of *ho, ho, ho*s that could charm any child's—or adult's—heart.

The kids burst out with cheers, and several moms who stood in line with their kids smiled at Brent, their eyes sparkling warmly. Miles looked up at Zoe, his mouth parted in surprise. And Prince, his tail wagging with excitement at the sound of his owner's voice, bounded over to Brent's side and sat beside the Santa mailbox, his reindeer antlers lopsided but staying on his head.

Scratching his fake beard with one hand, Brent opened the front of the large mailbox and gestured restlessly. "Santa's got a busy day, so hurry up and drop those letters in here, okay? Go on, kids. Hurry it up."

For over twenty minutes, Brent stood there, scratching as the line progressed forward, each child—and occasionally an adult—dropping their letter into Santa's mailbox. But through it all, he maintained his Santa voice and even cracked a smile.

Zoe ducked her head, hiding her own smile. She kissed a red curl on Holly's smooth forehead and whispered, "Maybe Brent has a little Christmas spirit buried in him somewhere after all…"

Chapter Five

"Don't ever ask me to wear this thing again." Brent yanked off the fake Santa beard as Zoe drove her Jeep up the driveway to her cabin. It took more effort to get the beard off than it did to put it on considering it had become plastered to his jaw by a mixture of heat and sweat as he'd manned the Santa mailbox for a seemingly unending line of kids. "This itchy thing wasn't part of our initial deal."

Miles, seated in the back seat beside Holly, whooped with laughter. "His face looks like a tomato."

Zoe glanced at Brent, her green eyes widening as she surveyed his face. "Um…are you allergic to anything? Like wool? Or—"

"Now?" Brent gaped at her. That unbearable itch was back—the one in his left armpit. "You ask me that *now*?"

"Well, we were in a hurry, and the thought didn't occur to me…not to mention that Santa suit has been in storage for a year." She looked suitably ashamed. "It probably has a hefty dose of dust on it. I thought you were itchy because of that."

An odd sound—similar to a growl—wrangled its way free of Brent's throat as he scratched. "And probably fleas from the feel of it."

Miles laughed. "There's no fleas in the cabin." His

laughter faded as Prince stuck his head over the back seat. A look of sheer happiness appeared on Prince's face as Miles patted his head, but disappointment laced Miles's tone. "We don't have a dog."

Zoe parked the Jeep and narrowed her eyes at Brent. "I keep our cabin spotless and free of pests. And you know what? I think I resent your implica—"

"*You* resent?" Brent exited the Jeep, stalked to the back of it and opened the back door. "Come on, Prince. Home."

Prince sprang out of the Jeep, butted Brent's thigh, then padded over to Brent's truck that was parked nearby.

"Wait." Zoe walked to the other side of the Jeep, opened the door and began unbuckling Holly from her car seat. "We already have a bag full of letters, so you can take your share now." She nodded toward the inside of the cab. "Miles, will you pick out a handful of letters for Mr. Carson?"

A muffled *yes, ma'am* along with the opening and shutting of a door, then Miles joined Brent at the back of the Jeep.

The boy looked up at Brent, his brows raised. "How many you want?"

Brent glanced at the large red Santa sack, stuffed full of Dear Santa letters, laying on the back floorboard of the Jeep. He shrugged, then scratched, eager to peel off the stifling layer of Santa suit. "Doesn't matter. A handful, I guess."

Miles untied the string on the bag, grabbed a handful of letters and handed the small stack to him. As Brent turned to leave, Miles held up his hand. "Wait. Your hands are bigger than mine." The boy dug back into the bag, scooped up another stack of letters and placed them on top of the others on Brent's palm. "There. Now your hand's full."

No doubt. "Thanks." Brent walked away, and after three long strides across Zoe's driveway, he sat in the cab of his truck, Prince and the stack of letters by his side, and cranked the engine.

Someone knocked on the driver's window.

He glanced to his left, sighed at the sight of Zoe and her pink stocking cap and rolled down the window. She held Holly, who slept in her arms. The baby's pink cap had slipped behind her ears, leaving her downy red hair to ruffle in the cold breeze.

Brent had a strong urge to reach out, cup his palm over the baby's red curls and protect her forehead against the wintry wind, but he turned away instead, his strong jaw clenching as Zoe's graceful hand curved around Holly's cheek in much the same way he would've done.

"Look, I know today wasn't exactly fun for you," Zoe said softly. "But thank you for helping. It meant a lot to me, Miles and Holly, and I know God would be pleased."

"Why would I want to please Him?" Heat scalded Brent's face as the angry words burst from his lips.

Zoe hesitated, and the feel of her intense scrutiny made his face flame even hotter. "You made today special for a lot of kids, Brent," she said softly.

He couldn't respond. His throat had tightened at the thought of his own newborn baby girl. Her hair had been brown and not nearly as thick as Holly's, but she'd been beautiful. He hadn't held her that fateful day six years ago. Not even to say goodbye. The loss of both her and Kayla had been too painful.

He should've held her. And he shouldn't have spoken such harsh words about God.

Zoe smiled. "As a matter of fact, you made a great

Santa. I think for a moment there, you may have actually enjoy—"

"Gotta go." He cranked the engine and shifted into
reverse, speaking over the truck's growl. "I'll write responses to the letters and drop them off within the next
day or two."

Brent hit the gas pedal, backed swiftly out of the driveway and accelerated down the highway. He lifted his hot
face into the frigid wind that whipped through the open
window and tried not to think of the wounded look on
Zoe's face as she'd stood in the driveway, cradling Holly,
watching him drive away.

That night Brent emerged from a cold shower feeling
refreshed and rejuvenated. Although it was impossible not
to feel better after peeling off the sweaty Santa suit, scrub-
bing every inch of his itchy, overheated skin and dousing
himself with frigid water for almost an hour.

Rubbing a towel over his wet hair, he left the bathroom
and ambled downstairs in a pair of warm sweatpants and
a T-shirt. Prince was waiting by the fireplace, where a
fire Brent had built an hour earlier had burned down into
smoldering coals.

"Sorry, boy." Brent rubbed Prince's head as he walked
by toward the front door of his cabin. "I'll grab some
more firewood, and you'll be warm and cozy again before you know it."

After donning his coat, retrieving more firewood and
stoking the fire, Brent resumed his nightly routine. He
brewed a fresh carafe of coffee, poured a hefty serving
into a mug and sat at his desk by the large picture window in his living room. There were no clouds and the sky
was clear, exposing thousands of bright stars that sparkled

down at him. He turned on the small lantern that was positioned on one side of the desk, closed his eyes and tried to picture Kayla.

He tried to imagine her long dark hair—the way it had rippled across her shoulders as she'd turn her head, the feel of the silky strands gliding between his fingertips. He tried to remember her smile, tried to hear the joyful sound of her laugh and tried to feel the way her serene presence used to surround him, putting him at ease.

But the thoughts wouldn't come.

Frowning, he opened a drawer, pulled out a blank sheet of stationery, placed it on the desk and picked up a pen. Then he closed his eyes and tried again.

Still, the vivid memories he'd preserved, protected and relived for six years wouldn't come.

Heart pounding, he stood and began pacing, striding across the living room floor. After a few minutes, he sat down again, picked up his pen and wrote, his hand trembling.

My dearest Kayla,

He sat there, memories of Kayla finally flickering through his mind. But none of the fleeting memories were an image of her smiling face, the sound of her sweet voice or the feel of her comforting touch. Instead, he saw only her hands. Her small palms testing the sturdiness of Christmas tree branches, her long fingers slipping the delicate strings of ornaments onto the evergreen tips of a live Christmas tree and her soft fingertips flipping delicate pages in her turquoise Bible to 2 Corinthians 9:15—familiar actions she undertook every Christmas. Though the rest of her was out of reach of his mind, he could see each movement of her hands clearly, as though she sat right beside him, her hands the only part of her within his view.

Squeezing his eyes shut tighter, his mind and heart strained to revisit her fully, to picture the very essence of her in full, physical form as he'd known her. But no matter how hard he tried he couldn't see her face. The memories wouldn't come—only her hands and their purposeful movements would spring to mind.

He tossed the pen onto the desk, thrust back his chair and shot to his feet. "Are you punishing me again?" He looked up, glaring at the wood beams of the ceiling and envisioning the night sky beyond. "Trying to take every bit of her away from me?"

Silence descended over the room.

"Zoe said you'd be pleased with what we did today." He looked down at his hands, hanging limply by his sides. "Are you?" he whispered. "Is that really what you want from me right now?"

A log popped in the fireplace, drawing his eyes toward the other side of the room where the Santa suit lay crumpled on the floor after he'd thrown it down carelessly moments after arriving home earlier that evening. The flames of the roaring fire flickered, casting a bright glow across the room, and the firelight seemed to flicker intensely on the Santa suit and Dear Santa letters he'd placed on his desk when he'd returned home earlier.

He stared at both. His eyes moved from the stack of letters on the desk to the Santa suit resting on the floor, then back again. A sense of dread washed over him, and he jerked into motion, striding across the room, snatching up the Santa suit from the floor and carrying it through to the bathroom. He filled the large, ceramic tub with cold water and a small amount of detergent, plunged the bright red coat then pants into the soapy water and scrubbed for over half an hour, working the tension from his limbs and easing the tremors rattling his frame.

He hand-washed the beard last, and by that time, his nerves had settled enough that he could handle the fragile material more gently. He took his time, smoothing the long white strands of the beard beneath the soapy water with his thumbs, gently squeezed the excess water from the long white strands, then hung it over the shower rod beside the Santa coat and pants to dry.

His heavy breaths slowing, he walked back into the living room and stared at the stack of Dear Santa letters on the desk.

"It's just today," he whispered to Prince. "That's all. We just had an unusual day."

Prince didn't respond. The pup lay motionless by the fire, only his belly lifting and rising slowly on each of his low, contented snores as he slept.

Brent returned to his desk. He sat, picked up the stack of letters and stared at the handwriting on the front of the first envelope. The letters were scrawled in an uneven line, each letter of the words a different size, clearly written by a child.

He glared down at the letters, wanted to throw them outside, let them freeze against the hard ground overnight then wilt in the cool mix of morning mist and weak rays of sunlight.

It was disgusting—this feeling inside him. This abhorrent disdain for something so hopeful and cheery. The innocent wishes of children should be cherished rather than cruelly dismissed.

Who was he? He didn't know this stranger—this cruel person—he'd become. But the pain inside him had grown so dark and heavy over the years that it had smothered his goodwill and buried the man he used to believe himself to be.

It'd be easy to drive back to Zoe's cabin, return the letters and shirk this obligation. But he'd made a deal—an agreement of good faith that the strong Christian man he'd once been would've honored—and he'd see it through.

He slid the lone sheet of stationery addressed to Kayla to the side, placed the stack of Santa letters in front of him and opened the top one. He read through several, each one written by a child, the requests all pretty much the same: a bike, video game, money, teddy bear or football. Each letter was full of excited anticipation and expectations that their greatest wishes would be fulfilled by the big-bellied man they believed would shimmy down their chimneys on Christmas Eve.

Brent rubbed his temples where a painful throb had begun. He supposed this should help lighten his mood. It was the Christmas season after all. A time when bright lights, colorful decorations and cheerful good wishes from strangers should lift a man's spirit and inspire cheer and goodwill within his soul.

But he wasn't happy. The prospect of bubbly grins and a festive mood made him sadder than ever. And the thought of it—the mere thought of what a cynical man he'd become—scared him.

His resolve wearing thin, he opened one more letter. His hands stilled around the crumpled piece of notebook paper that had clearly been wadded up and smoothed out more than once during its composition.

Dear Santa,
This is Riley Jenkins. I'm a 11 year old girl and I live on 572 Beauchamp St. It's the house with the blue door. The turquoise one that sticks out.

This is stupid.

I know you don't exist. I know you're just some stranger reading my letter because it's like your duty, or something. I'm only writing this because it's required for class. I have a little sister and I get extra credit in English if I help her write her own letter to Santa and write one myself too. I want a good grade, so I guess I'll write something to make this worth your while. Whoever you are.

My dad died last year.

That's it. That's what broke my family. And I know you can't make it right.

My mom took on a second job but she still can't pay the bills. She told me yesterday that we have to move soon. I don't want to. Everything in this house reminds me of my dad, even that dumb blue door he spent a whole Saturday painting three years ago. He thought it was tacky but did it for my mom because he knew it was her favorite color. That's the kind of man he was. He loved us that much.

I get it. Houses cost money and we don't have it. We're gonna have to move. But it'd be nice to have one last Christmas in this house. My Dad's kind of Christmas that'll make my mother smile and my sister happy. One last time. In this house with memories of my dad.

He's the one who put up our Christmas tree every year. A live one with blue ornaments that matched my Mama's favorite door. He'd set it up on the front porch where everyone could see it. Mom would walk past it every morning on her way to work and smile. That made me smile too. My dad loved my mom and made her happy.

*Could you do that? Make my mother feel loved
again? Make us all feel happy again?*

*I doubt it. Because you don't even exist, do you?
You're just some silly thing someone made up to
make kids think the world is good and that everything is going to be okay and that if you just wish
for something, you can have it. But that's not how
it works, is it?*

*I'm sorry. This isn't your fault. Whoever you are.
I should just ask for a new cell phone or something
because it's Christmas and I should be happy. But
I'm not. I don't think I ever will be again.*

I'm sad every day.

Brent laid the letter on the desk and smoothed it with
his palms, his trembling fingertips stumbling over the
wrinkles in the page. He wanted to reach through the
crumpled paper to the broken-hearted little girl on the
other side, take her hand in his and tell her she wasn't
alone, that the colorful lights and jovial voices surrounding him made the darkness inside him bleaker, too.

But he also wanted to tell her something else. Something that surprised even him.

He wanted to tell her that there was more out there
than the grief she was feeling. There were pink stocking caps with bells and bows, German shepherds with
reindeer antlers, curious little boys who caused trouble
without meaning to, cute babies with downy red hair and
generous, caring people like Zoe who dedicated her life
to making the lives of others better.

Good things that God sometimes blessed people with that
would lessen—however briefly—the ache in their souls.

Riley Jenkins was so young. There was so much more

left in life for this little girl to look forward to. So much joy waiting for her in the future.

Brent opened a drawer, retrieved a fresh piece of stationery and began to write.

"We won't think of him."

Seated on a kitchen barstool in her cabin, Zoe adjusted Holly more comfortably against her left shoulder and patted her little back gently. Holly had eaten a lot this morning, having slept deeply for almost six hours straight last night, not rousing until the early morning hours.

As it was Monday, Zoe had had to leave Holly with Jessie two hours ago in order to drive the foster children who resided at Hummingbird Haven to school in the colorful van that belonged to the shelter. There'd been eight children dressed in warm coats, colorful scarves and fuzzy mittens on board, Miles choosing to sit in the seat directly behind Zoe as she drove, and they'd all been excited about the merry season and holiday festivities their teachers had planned for them at school, chatting cheerfully about their daily happenings.

Every day, the student choir practiced holiday songs and each class of students rehearsed their part in the elementary's school-wide Christmas play. There would be a holiday gala in three weeks for parents to see their children perform, an end-of-the-semester holiday party on the last Friday of school before Christmas, two weeks of holiday vacation right after and, most importantly it seemed, an endless wish list of presents that may or may not appear under each child's Christmas tree on Christmas morning. Laughter and whispers peppered the air in the van as Zoe had driven, assisted them off the van and waved them on to a productive day.

Normally that was the part of day Zoe enjoyed the most. Mornings were always a fresh start full of endless possibilities, and usually on the drive home, she'd swing by the local coffee shop, order a sugary coffee, then drive home while sipping it slowly and thinking of each child settling into their classrooms, logging into their laptops or opening books and starting their day with a smile. And she'd pray silently on the way back to her cabin that each child's day would end just as joyfully as it had begun.

Today, though, she hadn't stopped for coffee and she'd barely managed to finish her daily prayer before her mind drifted elsewhere. To a soulful pair of brown eyes, a stubborn-set mouth and a handsomely brooding expression, to be exact.

"We won't think of him," Zoe repeated, rubbing Holly's back again. "I promised I wouldn't barge into Brent's life anymore, and I won't. Brent's emotions and what he does with his days are no longer my business." She grimaced. "Not that they ever were to begin with."

But she couldn't quite get the image of Brent's face last night as he'd driven away from her cabin out of her mind…or heart. She'd thought yesterday's activities—Brent dressing as Santa, assisting with the installation of the Santa mailbox and greeting the eager kids in the town square—would have brightened his mood. But after returning to her cabin, he'd seemed angrier than ever. Grief had hung over him like a shroud when she'd spoken of God being pleased. It had clouded his eyes, sagged his shoulders and hardened his tone.

Why would I want to please Him?

Even though his abrupt dismissal of God had stung, she'd set it aside, only able to focus on the sadness that clung to him. She still wanted—more than ever, it seemed—to comfort him.

"It's none of my business," she said out loud, more firmly this time. "I suggested he answer Santa letters in hopes that will help him, but that's all I can do. All I should do. Because I'm no longer a barger, am I, Holly?"

An emphatic burp burst from Holly's lips, echoing around the empty kitchen. One much louder than any an infant her size should've been able to produce.

Zoe smiled. "Gracious! I can see you agree with me wholeheartedly." She patted Holly's back gently. "That's good, then. I needed the reinforcement." She inhaled deeply, cradled Holly more comfortably with one arm and retrieved an envelope from the stack of letters scattered on the kitchen table in front of her with the other. "Time to get back to work."

She tucked one end of the envelope under her chin, opened it with one hand, tugged out the letter and began reading.

> *Dear Santa,*
> *I know I'm post to ask for something, but I want to do a trade.*
> *I got a little sister. She's real little. Like, smaller than a football. She eats a lot and sleeps a lot and cries a lot. And her diapers stink.*

Zoe laughed and turned the envelope over. It was written by Kent Marsh, a seven-year-old boy who lived two blocks from the church she attended. She kept reading.

> *She's all right, I guess. But see, she can't do nothing. What I really want is a brother. A big one. One*

taller than me. One that can walk and talk and play games. One that doesn't stink or cry all the time.

Mom said she might can get me a new brother. Her and dad. But that it takes a long time to have a baby if God gives them one. And that maybe I could just have a new video game this year instead. But I'd rather have the brother. Ask God to make him tall and strong and funny, okay? And good at basketball. I'll trade you my little sister for him, and you can take her with you when you drop him off on Christmas Eve.

Oh, and could you make sure the teachers give us pizza at the end of year Christmas party? The pepperoni kind with lots of cheese. And grape soda instead of milk? And all different kinds of candy bars?
Thanks Santa,
Kent

"A trade, huh?" Zoe smiled and rubbed her forehead. "I don't know about Kent's wish, Holly. I can definitely provide pepperoni pizza and candy bars at the school's end-of-the-semester Christmas party, but the big brother… that one's gonna be kinda tough."

Someone knocked on the front door.

Zoe grinned. "Oh boy, Holly. Maybe that's the mailman with a gift from Santa? We could do with a dose of cheer around here today."

Even a Christmas card would be a blessing. Anything, really…so long as it wasn't a bill.

She slipped off the kitchen barstool and cradled Holly close to her shoulder as she walked across the living room and opened the front door.

Brent stood on the other side, a wrinkled piece of paper

in one hand, an envelope in the other and Prince panting happily by his side. "This one's important."

Zoe stared at him, the intense urgency in his dark eyes almost mesmerizing.

"Do you know Riley Jenkins?" he asked, holding the wrinkled piece of paper up a bit higher. The cold breeze outside picked up, ruffling his thick hair and flapping the paper about in his hand. "She needs help."

Zoe blinked, dragged her eyes away from the determined set of his attractive mouth and huddled Holly closer to her neck, blocking her tiny body from the wintry wind gusting into the living room. "I...well, I know Riley's younger sister, Kate. She's in Miles's class and lost her father recently."

Brent, holding her gaze intently, pressed the letter against the back of her hands which cradled Holly. "You need to read it." He glanced at Holly and blushed—he actually blushed!—then stepped back and lowered his hand. "I'm sorry." He spread his hands, eyeing Holly. "I didn't mean to barge in on you and Holly like thi—"

"Barge?" Zoe shook her head, the eager purpose in his handsome expression kicking her heart rate up a notch. "No, you're not barging. Not at all." The uplifting energy exuding from him was more than welcome. She stepped back and waved one arm toward the interior of her cabin. "Please, come inside out of the wind."

He did, and Prince followed close to his heels, the pup's tail wagging with excitement as his gaze darted around the room. Zoe shut the door, shivering as the last bit of cold air dissipated among the warmth in the cozy living room.

"Is it okay for Prince to be in here?" Brent asked, pointing at the German shepherd. At her nod, he continued, "I wrote Riley back. But I feel like we should do more."

"Okay." Zoe nibbled her lower lip. "I'll read her let-ter…and yours if you'd like me to? You know, just to get a sense of how to help her in the best way possible."

Brent hesitated and looked down at the wrinkled page he held as well as the envelope in his other hand. "Yeah. I guess that'll be okay." He glanced at Holly, who was still comfortably resting against Zoe's shoulder. "Would you like me to… I don't know, hold her?" He shrugged. "While you read, I mean."

Zoe grinned. "Like a trade?"

The tension in his muscular frame eased slightly as he chuckled. "Yeah." The left corner of his mouth lifted in a boyish smile. "I guess so. If it's okay with you? I'll be careful with her."

"I know you will," Zoe said softly. "Would you feel more comfortable sitting on the couch or a stool at the kitchen table?"

He glanced around, looking at the stools surrounding the kitchen island, then watched Prince roam around the living room, sniffing at each foreign object. "The couch will work best, I suppose."

Zoe smiled. Despite his confident posture, his deep voice shook just a bit and two lines of nervous strain bracketed his mouth. "Take your time getting settled. Hol-ly's not going anywhere."

It took a few minutes for Brent to get comfortable on the end of the couch, placing the letter and envelope to the side on the cushions and setting his arms just right to receive the infant. He stiffened when Zoe lowered baby Holly into his arms but relaxed back against the cushions once she was safely settled within the crook of his elbow.

The boyish smile he'd flashed earlier returned, grow-ing just a smidge as he gazed down at Holly…almost in wonder. "She's like a feather, isn't she? I can barely feel her in my arms."

Holly's wide eyes focused on Brent's face, a soft coo escaping her as she stared up at him, her eyelids growing heavy.

"Yeah," Zoe whispered, her vision blurring. "Her tummy's full, so she'll probably be asleep in no time."

She blinked rapidly, beating back the tears in her eyes, then scooped up the wrinkled letter and envelope Brent had set aside and sat in a nearby recliner. She read Riley's letter, each word evoking a fresh sheen of tears that replaced the ones she'd just forced back. There was so much sadness and despair in the girl's words. The same desolate tone in her letter that tinged Brent's voice at times.

"Gracious." She cleared her throat. "I think it's a good idea to touch base with the school counselor. I know her well and can ask her to check in on Riley. It might help her heal to talk things out with someone who's patient and caring."

Brent didn't answer. Instead, his burly upper body moved gently in a rocking motion, his attention focused on Holly's face as she blinked up at him sleepily.

Zoe set Riley's letter aside, opened the envelope and read the letter Brent had written to Riley.

Dear Riley,

I'm so sorry you lost your father. More sorry than I can say.

I wish I could send him back to you, take away your pain and put things back the way they used to be. But you're right, I can't.

What I can tell you, though, is that your father is still with you and always will be—every day. He lives in your heart, your mother's heart and your sister's heart. And his memory will always thrive there, no matter where you live. Your surroundings may change, but your dad will always be there to see and experience it with you because he left behind the best part of him in you. He's part of you and will live on through you. Our futures may change, but our pasts—the good parts of our past—we can carry with us no matter where we go.

Your love for your family is powerful. I assure you that your and your sister's health and happiness—the very sight of you—brings your mother more joy than you could ever know. A mother's love and strength for her children is even greater than you might imagine.

A wonderful future lies ahead of you, one full of possibilities and achievements that are limited only by your dreams. But for now, please do me a favor? Please look for the good—for good people and good blessings among the everyday mundane. Good is all around you. And cherishing—celebrating—the good memories with those you love, no matter how difficult it may be to do right now, will help you see and believe in the good that awaits you.

Look for the good...especially on the saddest days. Love, Santa

Zoe's lips trembled. She touched her fingertips to her mouth and continued staring down at the letter in her hands silently.

"Is it...okay?" Brent asked quietly. "I wasn't sure how a Santa letter should—"

"It's from the heart, Brent." She smiled at him. "I think it's just right."

When her eyes met Brent's, he ducked his head sheepishly as though embarrassed, saying softly, "I want to help her. Like you wanted to help me, I suppose."

"How?"

"I washed the Santa suit last night." He lifted his head, a small grin appearing. "There are tons of trees behind my cabin, and Riley's address is on the letter."

Zoe smiled wider, eyeing the tender way his big palm cradled Holly against his muscular chest. "What did you have in mind?"

Chapter Six

◦≈❧

Brent knew exactly what he had in mind to help Riley Jenkins: find a live tree with full branches on all sides at the perfect height to fit onto her front porch. Only, as he walked along the trail behind his cabin the next afternoon, he hadn't expected the woods to feel so strange without Kayla walking ahead of him, leading the way. But at least they weren't as dark and dismal as they'd appeared to him in the years past when he'd drummed up enough courage to venture down the same path he and Kayla had traversed together each year in the past to find a Christmas tree.

And this walk certainly wasn't as quiet—quite the opposite, in fact—considering Zoe, in her pink stocking cap with bells jangling, had been chatting unceasingly beside him from the moment their feet had hit the dirt trail behind his cabin.

"I'm so excited you suggested this," she said, her pink hiking boots crunching on acorns as she stepped carefully over knotted roots that protruded from the dirt along the trail. "I think Riley is going to be bowled over when she sees a Christmas tree on her porch. And you have so many." She splayed her arms out to either side, her palms lifted up toward the treetops as though each branch were laden with diamonds rather than pinecones. "These trees are so gorgeous! I mean, imagine having your own Christmas tree farm right behind your house."

Branches of the surrounding Leyland cypress and fir trees rose in the late afternoon wind as though puffing out their evergreen chests with pride.

Brent tucked his chin against the collar of his jacket to hide his grin. "This isn't a Christmas tree farm. It's just the woods."

"Perfect woods where God perfectly planted perfect trees that are perfect for Christmas!" Zoe's brows raised. "I think you're hiding one of Hope Springs's most precious jewels. God put these trees here for a reason, you know."

Brent laughed. "Yeah. To produce oxygen and support life. Not to be cut down in their prime and draped with commercialized goods."

Zoe pursed her lips. "You know what, Brent? You can be a real killjoy when you want to be." She raised her pink-gloved fists in the air and shook them. "Christmas is a time for celebration. A time to cheer over the fact that Jesus was born! What better way to do that than to partake in a centuries-old tradition that brings joy to others' hearts? And I'll have you know, everyone in Hope Springs who has them recycles their live trees. Hope Springs residents always do their part to take care of these mountains and help them thrive for future generations."

Brent smiled and shook his head. "If you say so, Zoe."

"Yep." She grinned up at him, the bells on her stocking jingling. "I do say so." She glanced around. "But what about Prince? Didn't you want to bring him on the adventure?"

"Nah. He gets wound up when we venture out here. All the new sights, sounds and smells…he'd take off first thing, and it'd take ages to round him up again." He shook his head. "I fed him extra well, and he's snoring his head off in the cabin."

They continued on, walking at a steady pace down the dirt trail that curved around the mountain beside Brent's cabin. The bright sun had dipped below the thick tree line and a cold wind swept through the trees, bending their branches and rustling the underbrush tangled around their trunks.

"I feel so guilty," Zoe said. She rubbed her gloved hands together and shrugged deeper into her warm winter jacket. "I mean, I know getting a babysitter for Holly and Miles was the right thing to do because it's too cold to bring Holly outside while we trek through the woods and Miles has school tomorrow, so it didn't make sense to keep him out late on a school night—especially considering we're out on an undercover mission."

Brent smiled wider when she stopped talking long enough to catch her breath. "I wouldn't call putting a Christmas tree on a kid's front porch at night an undercover mission. I'd say it's an anonymous good deed performed under the concealing cloak of darkness."

Zoe bumped him with her elbow and winked. "You've got a way with words. But an undercover mission sounds much more intriguing, don't you think? And it's always exciting to have a little good-natured mischief at Christmas. So long as the mischief helps others, which is exactly what we plan to do."

Brent studied her face, admiring the teasing light in her green eyes, pretty blush on her wind-chapped cheeks and bright smile full of enjoyment. "You really get into the holiday thing, don't you?"

Zoe grinned. "God's love is *the* reason to celebrate. Christmas is indeed the most wonderful time of year!"

"For some." He tore his attention away from the appealing glow in Zoe's expression and focused on the dark shadows that began to settle between the trees ahead. He shoved one hand into his pocket and gripped the large saw he carried tighter. "Those like Riley, who've lost loved ones, find it much harder to appreciate the cheerful glow of Christmas. It's hard to celebrate with light and laughter when you don't feel the same on the inside."

At least, that was how he felt.

Oh, he appreciated the season. He'd always been—and always would be—grateful for the tremendous gift God had given. But he was also acutely aware of what God had taken from him.

Even now, a day later, he could still feel the slight weight of baby Holly in his arms. He hadn't planned on offering to hold her—hadn't even wanted to, really, but the opportunity had arisen in Zoe's cabin and something inside him had compelled him to offer. And when Zoe had lowered Holly onto the crook of his elbow a bittersweet peace had washed over him.

He hadn't expected that. He'd expected the same gut-wrenching despair he felt anytime he thought of the baby girl he'd lost to overtake him. To feel bitter and possibly resentful of the child that lay in his arms.

Instead, a strange sense of contentment had bloomed in his chest as he'd thought of what it might feel like to be a father. If he'd had the opportunity to be a dad, to hold and care for a little girl like Holly or Riley. To protect her, teach her and support her as she grew into an adult, remaining in the background of her life for years to come, ready to support her should she call.

It had been an odd—and scary—experience to feel such hope at the possibility of being able to become a father again in the future, when he should've been bitter and angry at the reminder of what he'd lost.

Afterward, guilt had consumed him…as though he'd somehow betrayed the daughter he'd lost. And possibly Kayla.

"Any word on Holly's mom yet?" he asked quietly.

"No. Unfortunately Jessie and I have been unable to identify Holly's mother, and no one else has come forward to claim her." Zoe sighed. "Maybe I shouldn't have asked Jessie to watch Holly and Miles again. This is the second time in as many days that I've asked her to babysit, and she has a family of her own. I am Holly's and Miles's guardian. I should be the one sitting at home later tonight feeding and bathing Holly, reading a bedtime story to Miles and tucking them in to bed. But you had such a great idea, and I really wanted to be here and help you do this for Riley. And I can't be in more than one place at the same time. But still." She rubbed her forehead, frowning, then looked up at him, her wide green eyes apprehensive on his face. "Am I a bad foster mom?"

Brent's steps slowed as he stared down at her. He thought of how patient, kind and protective she always was with Miles. He thought of Holly in Zoe's arms, the way Zoe had looked standing in the living room of his cabin the day Holly had been left on his doorstep, cradling Holly close to her chest and smiling down at the infant. Then he recalled the caring way Zoe had hugged Holly to her chest, protecting her against the cold wind in her driveway after they'd returned from installing the Santa mailbox in Hope Springs's town square.

Zoe's blond hair, bubbly personality and outspokenness was infectious, and any child would be blessed to have her as a mom. The expression of love on Zoe's face whenever she looked at Miles and baby Holly was unmistakable.

It was the same expression Zoe usually had when she looked at...*him*.

Heart pounding, Brent stopped walking. "Why did you want to help me so much?"

Zoe, two steps ahead of him, drew to a halt and spun around, her brow creasing as she blinked up at him. "What do you mean?"

He couldn't answer, couldn't put words to what he really wanted to ask. But he needed to hear the answer just the same. He held her gaze, urging her to speak.

Mouth parting, she looked away. Her eyes roved over the trees that seemed to bend down and crowd in around them, obscuring the view beyond, hemming them in and making the world disappear.

"I..." She met his eyes again, a hesitant, almost frightened look in her own. "I care about you. Ever since the moment we met, I thought you were..." She closed her eyes, her chest lifting on a deep inhale, then she said softly, "I still think you're a good guy. More than that." She lifted her head, the fiery color in her cheeks spreading down her graceful neck. "I think you have a good heart underneath your, sometimes, less than friendly disposition." She bit her lip and lowered her head, dodging his eyes. "You're a wonderful man. And I know I've been nosy and noisy and barged into your life for years when you'd rather I didn't and that you barely knew I even existed before the past couple days, but—"

"I noticed you, Zoe." The words left his lips before he could think better of saying them. But that wounded look had reappeared on her face, the one he regretted putting there so many times, and it compelled him to speak. "I noticed you love helping others, especially kids. You go out of your way to help kids like Miles feel loved and valued. And you stop by Joe's Coffee Shoppe at eight every weekday morning after dropping off the foster kids at school, park that multicolored shelter van by the entrance and order the same thing every time—a large peppermint mocha with two shots of espresso, extra whipped cream and cinnamon dusting—even in the summer." He grinned, recalling the many times he'd sipped his coffee inside the coffee shop and looked out the window, watching her park. "You have trouble lining up that big van between the small lines and park crooked every time."

A small smile lifted one corner of her mouth.

"You've worn hot-pink hiking boots with white soles every time I've crossed paths with you on the hiking trails," he continued. "And every time you pass a low branch, you always reach up and tap it. You have a mother and sister who still live in your hometown, but you only go back to Alabama to visit them for Christmas once every three years because you can't bring yourself to leave your foster kids more often than that. You told me that once in the hardware store, two years ago, when you cornered me in the aisle, pretending to need a nail gun."

Her smile fell and her expression turned blank—almost detached.

"When you get angry or…" He pulled in a deep breath. "When someone says something that hurts you, you don't hurt them back. You speak the truth and keep trying to help in any way you can, whenever you can." He smiled. "I've never met anyone with a heart more generous than yours."

She licked her lips, then asked, "You…you noticed all that?"

"Yes," he said softly. "However unpleasantly I've behaved toward you, I want you to know that. I *have* noticed you, but I… I'm married." He winced. "Or I was. Until six years ago. But it doesn't feel like six years ago to me. Even though I lost her before you and I met, I still—" His breath caught. "I know that's hard for most people to understand, but… I'm not ready to let Kayla go. And with all the time we're spending together lately, I wanted to make that clear because the last thing I'd ever want to do is hurt you again."

Zoe's chin trembled, and she looked toward the trees, the tears gathering on her lower lashes making his chest ache. "You don't have to worry," she whispered. "I understand. I know we're working on this volunteer project as neighbors." She faced him again and smiled. It didn't look quite sincere but stayed firmly in place as she spoke her next words. "I know I'm only a friend."

Brent stared down at his boots. A heavy weight lifted from his shoulders at having this out in the open. There would be no misunderstandings, and hopefully he'd be more at ease working closely with her, knowing he wasn't leading her on unintentionally, having been honest and open. But a different sense of pain enveloped him. One he hadn't anticipated or felt before.

It settled deep inside his chest along with guilt for wanting this conversation to be different. For wanting to move on and allow himself to fall in love again…with *Zoe*.

"No," he whispered. Raising his head, he allowed himself to admire, for a very brief moment, how adorable she was. How compassionate, generous and kind. "In answer to your question, you're not a bad mom. You're a fantastic mom. I've noticed that, too."

I noticed you, Zoe.

Zoe sat in the passenger seat of Brent's truck, clasping her gloved hands in her lap and trying her best to look as though their conversation hadn't affected her in the slightest.

She thought she had succeeded, considering she'd managed to continue trekking down the trail through the woods, helped scout out a six-foot cypress that was a vibrant green with full branches, assisted Brent in sawing it down, hefted it back up the trail and loaded it in the bed of his pickup truck. And she'd even kept a pep in her step as they'd shopped in a Christmas décor store in the town square for the perfect shade of blue ornaments to decorate Riley's tree. Through it all, she'd remained cheerful, patient and calm, giving the outward appearance of a woman who was completely at ease with being just friends with Brent Carson. And for the duration of the drive from the Christmas décor store to a nearby neighborhood in Hope Springs, she'd continued the charade and smiled peacefully, conversing with ease in the cab, glancing nonchalantly in Brent's direction occasionally as he'd navigated the truck toward Riley Jenkins's house.

She'd had to work extra hard, though, to force herself not to recall the warm, concerned tone of his voice as he'd spoken to her in the woods behind his cabin. Or to dwell on the tender expression that had appeared on his face as he'd peered intently into her eyes even as he'd gone out of his way to clarify that their relationship had not changed. That they were just neighbors—possibly friends—but nothing more, no matter how much time they spent together during this volunteer holiday project.

I'm not ready to let Kayla go.

Zoe squeezed her eyes shut, holding her breath as a sharp pain gnawed her stomach and a fresh set of tears welled under her lashes, threatening to spill down her cheeks.

"You okay?"

At the deep throb of Brent's voice, Zoe turned her head and stared out the passenger window, blinking hard against the hot moisture in her eyes. To distract herself, she focused on the magnificent night sky overhead, filled with the bright stars and a crescent moon that, despite its slim shape, cast a cozy glow over the mountain range in the distance.

This was not a time for tears. It was a time to brighten Riley Jenkins's Christmas.

"Of course." Tears gone, Zoe faced Brent and summoned a bright smile. "I was just thinking."

He frowned, the concerned expression she'd glimpsed on his face earlier in the woods returning to his face. "About what?"

She smiled wider. "About why you agreed to wear the Santa suit but not the pillow." She looked pointedly at the flat expanse of his middle. "I mean, you're wearing the suit, so it makes sense that you should stuff the pillow under your jacket as well. Santa's not skinny, you know? He eats a lot of Christmas cookies, and lots of Christmas cookies make for a big belly."

Brent rolled his eyes, but a smile flitted across his mouth. "Look, the only reason I chose to wear this thing tonight is because I want this good deed to be inspiring. I don't want Riley peeking out her window and seeing some strange man putting a tree on her front porch. If she does sneak a peek and she catches us in the act, I'd rather she catch a glimpse of Santa and an elf. That way there'll still be some mystery about who gave her the tree."

"She's eleven. And from what I read in her letter, she gave up on the idea of Santa quite some time ago."

"Yes, but—" Brent held up one finger as he slowed

the truck down a narrow street "—that doesn't mean we shouldn't at least try to put a little holiday joy in this. It's like you said—there are times when surrounding people with cheerful lights and decorations might lift their spirits. Not necessarily everyone's," he clarified, "but maybe there's a better chance that the holiday joy might improve an eleven-year-old's outlook a bit."

Zoe considered this silently, thinking of the grief-stricken expression on Brent's face as he'd spoken of his late wife. He'd said most people wouldn't understand why he wasn't ready to move on after six years. But she did. She understood perfectly. Brent was exactly the man she'd imagined he was when she'd first met him—a good man who loved deeply and faithfully. That was one of the many qualities she'd grown to value about him over the years.

But even though she understood and appreciated why he held on to the memory of the life he'd enjoyed with his late wife, she couldn't quell the swell of disappointment that moved within her at the thought of Brent never loving another woman again. Never emerging from his grief long enough to care for another woman—possibly her.

She looked out the window again, peering at the houses they passed, disgust moving through her at the thought of her selfishness. She may never have Brent's heart, but she could still care for him as a friend. She should be grateful for that. Somehow.

"Oh, there's a blue door," Brent said, easing the truck to a stop beside the curb. "So does that mean this is the right place?"

Forcing her lovelorn thoughts aside, Zoe sat upright in her seat and craned her neck, scrutinizing the small brick house with blue door to their left. "Yes. 572 Beauchamp. That's the place." Excitement surged through her, and eager for a distraction, she rubbed her gloved hands together giddily. "All but two of the windows are dark, only the porch light is on and it's well after time for kids to be settled inside on a school night." She glanced behind her at the dim streetlights and empty road, then ahead where each house sat dimly lit and just as quiet as the ones beside them. "All's quiet on the Eastern and Western Fronts." She opened her door. "Let's go make Riley Jenkins's day—"

"Wait." Brent hunched over the steering wheel and narrowed his eyes at the front porch. "That porch is screened in, and there's a storm door." He glanced at her. "How are we going to get past that if it's locked?"

"I'll pick it."

Brent's brows rose. "You know how to pick a lock?"

"Not really." She grinned and tugged a bobby pin from the bottom of her pink stocking cap. "But going by what I've seen in movies, I have a lock-picking tool, and it can't be that hard, can it?"

The sarcastic disbelief in Brent's expression should have tempered Zoe's excitement. But thankfully undercover holiday missions, it seemed, had a unique side effect of reinforcing her self-confidence.

"I'm dressed the part," she said teasingly, gesturing to her costume. "And Santa's elves are capable of anything."

It took fifteen minutes of whispering, finagling and grunting in the frigid air to unload and carry the six-foot live cypress to the front steps of Riley Jenkins's front porch under the cloak of darkness.

"All right," Brent whispered. "Break out the bobby pin and do your thing."

Smiling, Zoe tiptoed over to the storm door, stuck her bobby pin into the lock carefully and grabbed the door's handle to steady herself. It swung open at her slight touch.

Her shoulders sagged, and the adrenaline rush she'd experienced subsided. "Aw, mercy. It's unlocked." She looked at Brent in disappointment, then a thought occurred to her, and she made a face. "Don't people know they should lock their doors?" she whispered. "Given the level of violent crime in today's society, it's prudent to lock doors and windows before you go to bed at night. If someone leaves their door unlocked, anyone can just—"

"Sneak onto their front porch and put up a Christmas tree?" Brent asked, arching one eyebrow. "Like us?"

"Yep." Zoe's grin returned. "Thankfully."

Thirty minutes later, the tree was up and decorated, no one had caught them in the act and the street was still silent.

Zoe gave Brent a thumbs-up and said in a hushed whisper, "Mission accomplished."

His dark eyes met hers as he leaned his head around the Christmas tree they'd decorated with the blue ornaments they'd purchased and smiled.

He actually smiled! Not one of his tired half smiles or little mocking ones he used to humor someone, but a full-blown happy smile. One full of joy and a bit of boyish mischief. The kind she'd only seen on Brent's face twice before, once when he'd discovered Prince the day she'd snuck him in his front yard and for a fleeting moment while he was playing Santa at the mailbox.

"You did a good night's work, elf," he whispered in his gruff Santa voice. "Now, let's make a clean escape."

They tiptoed off the front porch, dashed across the front lawn and climbed back into Brent's truck, shutting the doors quietly behind them. Then they burst out laughing, looked at each other, then laughed harder.

After a few moments, Brent sagged back against the

driver seat, leaned his head against the headrest and, still smiling that wide, handsome smile, chuckled even louder. His deep, appealing rumble filled the cab of the truck, warming Zoe's heart and tugging her mind back to all those wonderful qualities about him that appealed to her so much.

She adjusted the stocking cap on her head and smiled as the bells jingled, even though her heart broke a little bit more.

"Oh, man." Brent sighed. "This was fun. Thrilling, even." He glanced at the front porch, his eyes moving over the festive Christmas tree they'd decorated with bright blue ornaments that matched the front door perfectly. "It kind of amps you up, doesn't it? Makes you want to keep going. Makes you want to do more."

"I read somewhere that doing a good deed helps those who give as much—if not more—as those who receive."

"I think I could believe that." He faced her again, and the spark of joy in his expression made her long to reach out, cup his strong jaw and smooth her thumb over the full curve of his lower lip. "What about you?"

She froze. "What do you mean?"

"Are you tired?"

She shook her head.

He smiled wider. "What if we do yours?"

"Mine?"

"Yeah. I noticed when I was in your cabin that you decorated your mantel, but I didn't see a tree anywhere. You want to go pick one out from behind my cabin?"

"Oh, no. I have one already."

"Then how about when I drop you off at your place, I come in and help you set up your tree?"

"You…you want to help set up my Christmas tree?"

"Yeah." His smile slipped just a little. "Miles is probably in bed right now, right?" At her nod, he continued, "So I figure we put up your tree and decorate it tonight while he sleeps, and when he gets up in the morning, it'll be a nice surprise. Don't you think?"

Excitement exuded from his muscular frame in waves, making it difficult for her to speak. "I suppose it would be a nice surprise for Miles."

But Brent in her cabin? At night? With that handsome grin and excited expression? On the very same day he'd gone to great pains to explain that he just wanted to be friends?

She'd been looking forward to dropping the brave pretense when she got home, crying in the shower, stuffing her belly full of peppermint ice cream, then crawling under her flannel sheets and putting an end to today's humiliation of unrequited affection.

Zoe sank back against her seat, an odd combination of despair and exhilaration flowing through her veins at the idea of Brent standing by her side, decorating a Christmas tree and flashing his magnificent smile...his presence serving as a stark reminder of what could be if he cared for her in the same way she cared for him.

And what about Jessie? At this time of night, she would've already put Miles and Holly to bed, which meant she'd be waiting right now at Zoe's cabin for Zoe's return. What would she think of Zoe returning home with Brent in tow? Would Jessie think she was barging into Brent's life again? Being a barger? And worse, when Jessie asked the question she knew would inevitably come, how would she answer her?

Oh, Brent and I are just friends. He told me so earlier tonight. You know—that he still loves his late wife, isn't ready to let her go and wants to be sure I know I don't

stand a chance with him. But oh yeah, I accepted his offer
to set up my tree so I could spend more time with him and
pine away like a teenager with a crush.

Yeah...

For the sake of self-preservation alone, she should say
no. "Um, okay," she said, smiling. "Let's go to my cabin
and put up my tree."

The expression on Jessie's face when Zoe and Brent
entered Zoe's cabin said it all.

"You're here," Jessie said, turning off the TV and standing from her seated position on the couch. Zoe shifted from
one foot to the other as Jessie, a dumbfounded look on
her face, looked from Zoe to Brent, then back. "You're...
both here."

"Things went really well," Zoe said with a heavy dose of
forced cheer. "We snuck right up on Riley Jenkins's front
porch, set up the Christmas tree and slipped right off again
without anyone noticing."

Jessie continued to stare at the two of them. "I, well,
I'm glad to hear that."

Zoe cleared her throat, hoping the nervous tension rattling inside her didn't show on her face. "Brent asked if
he could stop by for a little bit." Her voice didn't emerge
quite as calm and unruffled as she'd planned. "He's offered to help me put up my Christmas tree."

Jessie's surprised gaze homed in on Zoe's face. "Oh,
really?"

Zoe shrugged, at a loss for words. Jessie's confusion
came as no surprise, and she could practically see the
gazillion questions forming behind her wide eyes, on the
verge of tumbling down to her open mouth.

"It's good to see you again, Jessie." Brent—bless him!—

eased around Zoe and offered his hand to Jessie. "I appreciate you taking care of Holly and Miles for Zoe tonight so she could help me do a good deed. And I know I shouldn't have barged in here so late at night, but I noticed Zoe hasn't put up her tree yet, and that's probably my fault. She's been spending time on cheering me and everyone else up and hasn't had time to spend on herself."

Jessie blinked several times, then smiled. "Oh, babysitting was no problem at all. My husband is taking care of our little ones, and Miles and Holly were absolutely perfect for me. They went right to sleep two hours ago." She shook his hand, then glanced over her shoulder around the living room. "But if you're helping Zoe put up her tree, you're in for a little surprise."

"How's that?"

Jessie laughed. "Well, for starters, Zoe has very particular tastes in her Christmas decorations and how they're arranged." Her smile grew. "She's fond of pink. As in Pepto Bismol pink."

Brent released her hand and pointed at the pink decorations on the fireplace mantel. "Like those?" He narrowed his eyes at Zoe. "You mean you don't use a live tree?"

Zoe blushed. "No. Trees don't grow in pink." She waved her hand in the air. "It's okay to be different. And anyway, what's wrong with pink? I happen to like pink, and this year hot pink is on trend for Christmas decorations. Pink symbolizes love, playfulness and nostalgia—all of which are perfect for the season. And, I might add, hot pink is a very festive color."

Chuckling, Brent glanced at the hot-pink garland hung on the fireplace mantel, then looked at the pink stocking cap on Zoe's head and smiled. "There's nothing wrong with pink, and it does suit you."

Jessie perked up at that, crossing her arms and raising her brows at Zoe, a teasing light entering her eyes. "Pink does look great on you, Zoe." She grinned at Brent, curiosity lighting her expression. "I take it you two had a good time on your Christmas mission? Will you two be doing more m—"

"It's getting late, and we've got lots to do in little time." Zoe looped her arm around Jessie's and tugged her toward the front door. "Thank you so much for babysitting, Jessie. I owe you a million favors already, but now you can say I owe you a million and one."

When they reached the front door, Zoe opened it and nudged Jessie out onto the front porch, whispering, "I'll call you later."

"But wait." Jessie held up her hand, rose to her tiptoes and craned her neck, peering over Zoe's shoulder toward the interior of the cabin. "This was his idea?" She moved closer, her eyes full of delight, and clasped both of Zoe's hands between her own. "I know I said you were barging when it came to him, but I'll be the first to admit I may have been wrong. He looks different. Not as brooding or grumpy somehow. I've never seen Brent smile like that. Maybe he's changed his mind, Zoe. Maybe he's coming around and taking an interest in y—"

"No." Zoe shuddered at the thought of telling the truth out loud. "He…he's just here to help me put up my tree, and that's it. He's being a good Christian tonight and doing good deeds. That's all."

"But Zoe—"

"Thank you for watching the kids, but I really have to go now." Zoe nudged her farther down the front steps. "I promise I'll call you later, okay?"

"Okay." Jessie, looking slightly disappointed, walked

down the front steps and onto the path that led to her cabin. After two steps, she turned back around and looked back at Zoe, her eyes expectant. "But you will call, right? I'm just dying to h—"

Zoe shut the door.

"Everything okay?"

Counting to three inside her head, Zoe summoned a cheery smile, then faced Brent. "Yep. I'm going to do a quick check on the kids, then I'll show you where that tree is."

Zoe checked on Holly and Miles, slipping silently into their rooms and peeking at their sleepy faces, using the few minutes to steel herself against the daunting task ahead.

"It's no big deal," she whispered quietly to herself. "We're just going to put up the tree, then he'll go home, and that's it."

Stealing one last glimpse at Miles, who slept peacefully in his bed, she slipped away again and reentered the living room.

"Is this where you usually put it?" Brent stood on the other side of the room, pointing to the left of the fireplace.

"Yeah." *Mercy, he looks gorgeous in the flicker of firelight.* "That's where it usually goes."

Twenty minutes later, she and Brent had hauled the tree from the attic, unboxed it and positioned it in a perfect spot beside the fireplace. They decorated it carefully using white-and-silver ornaments and ribbons Zoe had brought down from the attic and set at their feet.

Zoe worked hard to remain impersonal—or at least only friendly. She didn't focus on the warmth Brent's hand left behind when it brushed hers as they hung decorations on the tree limbs, didn't dwell on his masculine scent that appealed to her senses or the way his deep chuckle seemed to fill her entire living room with cheer. And she blushed only once when he smiled at her, the giddy light in his eyes that appeared when they'd completed their first good deed still shining bright as he decorated her tree.

She had done a pretty good job of just being a friend rather than a sappy admirer. That was until...

"You know what would hit the spot right about now?" Brent grinned. "A cup of coffee."

Zoe's eyes widened. "You...you want a cup of coffee? At this hour?"

"If you don't mind." His hands stilled in the act of positioning the last ornament onto a branch. "That is, if it's not too much trouble? I have a bit of insomnia and usually drink two or three cups every night. It's no big deal if—"

"No." She shook her head and smiled. "It's no trouble at all. But have you considered that all that coffee might be what's keeping you up?"

He grew silent, then said, "It's not the coffee."

When he didn't offer to explain further, she walked into the kitchen and went to work at her Christmas coffee bar. She brewed two single coffee pods and filled two mugs full of hot, aromatic coffee.

She removed the tops from the festively decorated glass canisters of condiments, then asked, "How do you take it?"

"Sweet, please." His deep drawl, sounding right behind her, made her jump. He leaned against the countertop nearby, surveyed her Christmas coffee bar and smiled. "You've got quite the setup here."

Hands trembling at the embarrassing reminder of the reason she'd acquired the coffee bar, Zoe spooned a hefty dose of sugar into each mug. "It was an impulse buy. I wanted something special for Christmas a few years ago. But I can never bring myself to dismantle it after the holiday ends. I just keep it like this all year." Her cheeks flamed, and she focused on the condiments instead, asking abruptly, "Maybe you should doctor yours yourself? You said you like it sweet, but I have a tendency to make it too sweet for most people."

"It's okay. I'll take it however you take it."

She paused, a small smile tugging at her lips despite her discomfort. "You sure, now? I tend to make my coffee rather…er, unique."

He laughed. "I'll take the chance."

"All right." She laughed. "You asked for it."

She added chocolate sauce, more sugar, a hint of cinnamon, mini marshmallows and several sprays of whipped cream, then handed one mug to Brent and grinned. "Go ahead. Give it a shot."

He did, staring down at the festive concoction before taking a slow sip, closing his eyes and groaning in appreciation—although he did flinch ever so slightly as the sweet concoction hit his tongue. "Best coffee I've ever had."

Zoe smiled back, the tender look in his eyes tugging her mouth into a deeper curve, stirring a light floating sensation throughout her limbs.

"Thank you, Zoe," he said softly. "I'm sorry I've kept you up so late, but doing a good deed made my insomnia a lot less painful tonight. I'm really glad you talked me into volunteering."

Her whole body seemed to sink deeper into the floor with each word he spoke. The hot mug she held burned the tender skin of her palms, but she tightened her grip on it, barely noticing. She reminded herself instead of the true reason for the task they'd undertaken.

"Doing God's work always lifts my spirits, too," she said. "Given the chance, He's able to lighten most of my burdens. Not always when I hope He will, but when He feels the time is right. So, I enjoy returning the favor for someone else when I can."

He looked down at his mug, his fingertips tapping the rim. "Do you speak to Him?"

She nodded. "Often."

"I stopped speaking to Him a long time ago." He glanced up, his dark eyes meeting hers. "Maybe I should try that again some time."

The vulnerability in his expression made her heart turn over in her chest. "Talking to God has always helped me. It wouldn't hurt to try."

Brent remained silent for a moment, then whispered, "One day, maybe." He took another sip of coffee, then asked, "You mind if I take a few more Santa letters home with me? It won't take me long to get through the ones I already have and since I'll be up tonight anyway, I might as well keep working."

"O-of course."

They finished their coffee, then Zoe sifted through a stack of Dear Santa letters on her kitchen table and handed Brent several. She walked with him to the front door and waved goodbye as he climbed into his truck and drove away.

Zoe shut the door, pressed her back against it and hugged her arms across her chest. She admired the perfectly decorated pink tree beside the fireplace, then glanced over at the two empty mugs sitting on the counter beside the Christmas coffee bar. She could still see Brent there, leaning lazily against the counter, sipping his coffee and smiling at her.

How perfect this night would have been if only he

would've said what she'd imagined him saying over the years in that very same spot. In that very same moment.

I'm glad we met.

Instead, she could only hear what he'd said on the trail in the woods behind his cabin.

I'm not ready to let Kayla go.

Chapter Seven

Two weeks later, Brent had slipped into a new routine and was surprised by how much he enjoyed it.

On Mondays, Wednesdays, Thursdays and Saturdays, he dressed as Santa and checked the Santa mailbox at Hope Springs's town square with Prince in his reindeer headband, Zoe and Miles—who wore their elf outfits— and baby Holly. It had been somewhat awkward at first, as Miles had not yet quite forgiven him for his rude behavior the day they'd first met. But after the first week of checking the mailbox together, Miles had begun to thaw a little. He'd even taken it upon himself to unlock the back of the old-fashioned red mailbox, pull out the letters in handfuls and dump them into the bag Brent held open beside him.

Brent and Miles chatted often as they worked, Miles sharing interesting stories from his days at school and Brent sharing details about his daily chores at the cabin that usually included chopping wood, making homemade syrup and spending time with Prince. And Prince, wearing the reindeer antlers Zoe had given him, seemed to be ecstatic when he sat, tail wagging, near Holly as though protecting her from the excited kids in line for their chance to visit Santa and drop their letter into the mailbox.

They'd all grown more comfortable spending time together at the Santa mailbox, and Brent's friendly, casual conversations with Miles seemed to please Zoe, who stood by smiling as she held baby Holly, watching them closely.

Zoe...

The more time he spent with her, the more he looked forward to seeing her again. Every hour he spent with her left his heart feeling a bit lighter—heady with joy, even. It surprised—and frightened—him...this new, powerful surge of longing.

He'd even begun to sleep again for several hours at night, thoughts of Zoe filling his mind when he closed his eyes and prompting him to spring to his feet the next morning when he woke, leaving him eager to begin answering a fresh batch of letters and preparing to perform a new round of good deeds. Her bright smile, carefree laugh and boisterous energy enticed him into enjoying the season a bit more every day.

Such as Tuesdays, when he read and answered letters from the Santa mailbox, and on Sundays, when he took a long hike along the trail behind his cabin with Prince. The fresh air and exercise did them both good. Prince enjoyed scouring every inch of the woodland territory with his curious nose and bounded between trees with abandon. And Brent enjoyed watching the German shepherd dart from the trail in pursuit of small critters, plundering through hedges, barking at birds and shuffling—nose to dirt— along the ground in search of new, interesting scents.

But something else happened on those leisurely strolls.

Brent found himself, more often than not, tilting his head back to watch the treetops sway in the breeze against the blue sky and whisper quiet questions to God, wondering how his heart could savor joy when it still harbored so much pain. And what role, if any, did God have in that?

The answers didn't come…but the anger he'd felt for years began to fade with each step as he continued along the path.

With each of his prayers, he was surprised to find his burdens grow a bit lighter…just as Zoe had suggested.

On Saturdays after performing as Santa by the mailbox in the town square, Brent pursued the same relief he found in prayer by performing more good deeds with Zoe. Then they'd head back to her cabin and spend time with Miles and Holly while having coffee. They'd had two more successful undercover holiday missions so far: one had been replacing a brokenhearted eight-year-old girl's stolen bike by soliciting donations from members in the community, and the second had been rescuing abandoned kittens from behind an eleven-year-old boy's home and relocating them to a local shelter for adoption.

Overall, Brent found he looked forward to every day of his new routine, but today was Friday. And Fridays… ah, Fridays were an absolute favorite—second only to his visits with Zoe, Miles and Holly on Saturdays.

First, he built a nice warm fire for Prince, who sprawled in his usual place on the carpet and thumped his tail excitedly against the floor even as his eyes grew heavy from the day's activities. Next, he brewed a fresh carafe of coffee, filled a mug, added two spoonfuls of sugar and garnished it with mini marshmallows that reminded him of Zoe, making him smile.

Finally, he walked into the living room, coffee in hand, sat at his desk by the large picture window and turned on his lantern. For a moment his hand hovered over the sheet of stationery he'd slid to the back corner of the desk over two weeks ago. The one that began, *My dearest Kayla…*

Brent stared at the greeting he'd written, then turned

away, picked up the stack of envelopes that rested on the opposite edge of the desk and sifted through the envelopes addressed with children's handwriting, his hands stilling on one that stuck out from the others.

This letter was folded neatly inside a long white business envelope rather than the small, colorful kind, and instead of the unsteady print of a child, this envelope was addressed neatly in cursive, by what looked to be an adult hand. It was from someone named Emmett Lee who lived at 721 Broad Oak Street in downtown Hope Springs.

Brent opened the envelope, withdrew the letter and began reading.

Dear Santa,

I'll be upfront with you. I am 82 years old, and although I know you don't really exist as an individual, I do still believe—even at my age—that the goodwill of Santa, the collected belief of children in your existence and the blessings of God working through you are still present and powerful.

So as unusual as it may be for someone my age to write to you, I do so in the belief and hope that what I ask for may actually come to fruition.

I've been blessed in many ways. I had a wonderful childhood with spectacular Christmases here in Hope Springs—oh, the stories I could tell!—a fulfilling career as a carpenter and I married my high school sweetheart sixty-two years ago. We bought a Victorian-style house and quickly turned it into our dream home—a home I still live in to this day.

But this house has grown quiet and doesn't glow with joy at Christmas like it used to.

I lost my wife to cancer 10 years ago, and though

we tried and hoped with all of our hearts, we were never blessed with children. I wonder how different this house would feel if my wife were still with me. How different it would sound if we'd been blessed with children and grandchildren. And I wonder what this house would look like from the outside if it were draped with gorgeous decorations and filled to the brim with children, family and friends on Christmas Eve or Christmas Day or any holiday.

I'm not normally a sentimental man, but I can't help but be envious of those who are happy around me. Those who are young, energetic and have a bright future to look forward to.

But for me...as time passes, I lose more than I gain.

I no longer have the strength to climb the stairs into the attic, pick up the boxes of Christmas decorations my wife kept there and carry them back downstairs. My arthritis makes it difficult to dress and cook, much less hang delicate Christmas decorations from tree limbs. My bad knees make it impossible to climb a ladder and string lights along the roof, and even if I could make it to the top rung, my vertigo wouldn't allow me to stay there safely for long.

Worse, I feel my mind slipping away from me a bit more each day. Things I could do in the past absentmindedly now take hours of concentrated focus to complete. When I look at photos of close friends I lost years ago, I can't remember their names and sometimes I don't recognize their faces. Some days are better than others, but I know eventually the days ahead will be different than any I've ever known.

The older I've gotten, the more I realize how far I've fallen behind. How slow I am and how much I hold others back. I've accepted that I won't be able to live independently for much longer. That I'll be a burden soon to someone. Something I dread and never want to be. But something that will inevitably occur should I live long enough.

I should be planning for the future, arranging my finances and reserving a room in an assisted living home, but I can't. I'm not ready to let go of the man I once was and the life I used to have.

Forgive me, please, for feeling sorry for myself. For being so cynical. I don't mean to. I try to keep busy, keep my spirits up and not complain. I have so much to be grateful for, have been blessed for so many years with so many good things, but the years have passed quickly and piled up sooner than I thought. I lost the fun, kind-hearted man I used to be before I noticed he'd slipped away from me. And now, more than ever, I find myself wishing...

Could you help me with one last wish, Santa? Could you help me bring joy, light, laughter and love to the gloomy halls of this old house one more Christmas?

Could you help me be seen as I used to be? The wise, energetic man I once was—not this aging stranger I don't really know?

Just once more, Santa. Please let someone see value in me.
With my greatest thanks,
Emmett Lee

Something tickled Brent's cheek, and he rubbed his face, realizing a hot tear was wetting his skin. He looked up, and his gaze moved to the picture window where the glow of the lantern cast his reflection on the glass pane.

He stared at his reflection and scrutinized his features one by one, searching for changes, noting fine lines that bracketed his mouth and crow's feet that fanned from the corners of his eyes. There were creases along his brow that had not been there six years ago.

He thought of Kayla, of all the happy years he'd had with her, and he thought of the six years since that he'd spent alone, bitter and angry, without her. Of what might have been had she and his baby girl lived.

He thought of the excitement and laughter he'd shared with Zoe during their Riley Jenkins Christmas Mission and the other good deeds they'd performed thereafter. He thought of the way Miles looked up at him by the Santa mailbox, smiling wide, and the feel of Holly's slight weight in his arms the day he'd held her in Zoe's cabin. Of the hope he'd felt at the prospect of being a father again and the eager way he'd begun to anticipate seeing Zoe each day.

Then he thought of Emmett Lee, sitting in his silent, empty house, grieving his losses and fearing the future, uncomfortable with the aging stranger he felt he'd become. Unable to let go of the past long enough to enjoy the present and face what may lie ahead.

Another tear followed the first, trailing over Brent's cheek, pooling into the corner of his mouth, then dripping off his chin. He wiped his face again, tugged his cell phone from his pocket and dialed. Someone answered on the third ring.

"Zoe," he asked softly, "is it okay if I come over?"

"Now? But I thought Saturday was y'all's usual get together?"

Zoe, standing at the kitchen island in her cabin, set her

cell phone on the counter, tapped the Speakerphone icon and said, "I know. But Brent's tone was kind of urgent when he called, so it must be important."

An exasperated sigh crossed the line—Zoe had expected as much—then Jessie spoke again. "So he wants to come over to discuss another Santa letter?"

"Probably, but he didn't say."

Zoe walked across the kitchen to the cabinets, opened a cabinet and grabbed a box of powdered sugar and a bottle of vanilla extract, then brought them back to the island and placed them on the counter beside a large mixing bowl and whisk. She tried to ignore the nervous tremor running through her at the thought of Brent entering her cabin again soon. Of his generous spirit filling every corner of her home while she did her best not to notice, or worse—admire, him!

"I'm guessing he wants to ask for advice on how to answer a letter, or maybe he's in the mood to do another good deed." She forced a cheery tone into her voice. "Who knows?" She opened another cabinet, grabbed a bottle of corn syrup and placed it beside the other ingredients on the counter. "Either way, it's a Friday night and there's no school tomorrow. Miles has finished his shower and is putting on his elf pajamas as we speak, Holly has been fed and burped and we'd already planned to frost a batch of Christmas cookies tonight, so the more the merrier." She moved to the other end of the kitchen island where Holly sat snuggled in her baby rocker, her wide, pretty eyes focusing on Zoe's face. "Isn't that right, sweet Holly? The more the merrier?"

Holly blinked, her rosebud mouth forming a cute little circle as she cooed up at Zoe.

"Is that our precious girl?" Jessie asked over the cell phone. "She's been anxious to talk lately, hasn't she?"

"Yep." Zoe smiled proudly. "Our baby girl started jibber jabbering a couple days ago. She's becoming a lot more vocal and a lot more demanding about when she receives her bottle." Zoe laughed, recalling Holly's frustrated grumbling earlier that morning while waiting to be given her breakfast. "But that's to be expected. She's hitting her milestones right on time."

"Because of you." A note of admiration entered Jessie's voice. "You've been so wonderful with her. And time is passing so fast. I can't believe how fast she's grown."

"I know. She's gained four pounds." Zoe tickled Holly's chin gently. "You're a strong little girl," she cooed to the infant, "aren't you?"

Holly cooed again, then gurgled in an attempt to speak, a tiny bubble forming on her lips.

Jessie laughter crossed the cellular connection. "Well, she's definitely not going to be a pushover with you raising her."

Zoe stilled, her fingertips skimming Holly's cheek as the baby moved her mouth and blinked up at her, trying to speak. "I don't know about that. I think I've become a bit of a pushover myself the past two weeks."

Static crackled over the speakerphone on Jessie's next words. "Has anything changed between you and Brent?"

Zoe fiddled with the whisk, spinning the handle between her thumb and pointer finger. "No. Nothing's changed since he gave me the 'friends talk.' Well, except for the fact that I moon over him a little more than I used to. Although I'm getting much better at hiding it, if I do · say so myself."

Zoe's cheeks heated. The day after Brent had helped

her put up her Christmas tree two weeks ago, Jessie had shown up at her door again and Zoe had shared everything. She'd even managed to repeat the words Brent had told her on the trail behind his cabin. And the look of dismay on Jessie's face upon hearing them had echoed the despair that still lingered within Zoe, making each subsequent visit with Brent more painful than the last.

"I know when we first talked about Brent that I suggested you help him in another way," Jessie said. "That you try to be a friend to him. But I may have given you bad advice. I think your invitation for him to volunteer with the Santa project this year was wonderful. But I never expected him to be so gung-ho or for him to dedicate so much of his time to his Santa role, and I especially never imagined him dragging you into every minute detail of the good deeds he cooks up. He's taking up so much of your time and—"

"I really don't mind," Zoe said quickly. "It's nice to have help answering the letters, and the kids really enjoy seeing Santa check the mailbox."

"I'm sure they do, but—"

"And Miles and Holly enjoy his company. They look forward to seeing him every time he comes over, and they just love spending time with Prince. You should see how good Prince is with Holly." She grinned. "He watches over that baby like she's his own pup."

"But is this really what you want?" Jessie asked.

Zoe bit her fingernail. "What do you mean?"

"I mean, isn't it difficult spending this much time with Brent? Him calling you so much and coming to your house? I know he's trying to help with the Santa letters and that he's enjoying this project, but you're changing, Zoe. You're not yourself lately. You don't have as much pep in your step and—as hard as it is to detect some-times," she said wryly, "I've noticed you're not as excited about the holidays." Her tone gentled. "Just the other day, you mentioned you weren't going to Alabama to visit your mom and sister this Christmas. But this is the third year since you've been, isn't it? Isn't this the year you'd nor-mally go home and spend Christmas with them?"

"Yes, but things are a little different this year. I have Holly and Miles to take care of. We haven't identified or found any of Holly's relatives yet…"

"And Brent is calling you now—almost every day, it seems—and you don't want to leave him." Silence fell for a moment, then Jessie said, "From what you told me, he knows how you feel about him. I'm glad he was hon-est with you about his feelings, but he leans on you too much and takes so much about you for granted. He's a good man, like you said, but I don't think he's considered how unfair he's being to you. Do you?"

"No," she whispered. "He hasn't."

Zoe rubbed the center of her chest, right where a per-manent ache had taken up residence. Over the past two weeks, she'd discovered that a heart could break more than once. Brent continued to break hers every time he smiled and laughed with her for hours, then said goodbye and walked away nonchalantly at the end of the evening… leaving her to mourn what might have been between them if he'd been able to see her as more than just a friend.

Though, to her knowledge, Brent had no idea how her feelings for him had grown. Now that she was spending so much time with him, getting to know him better, what had started out as a crush had developed into something more. She'd almost say that she pined for him. He had no idea how awkward and painful working in such close proximity with him could be. How much each of his handsome smiles, deep chuckles and caring interest in each of the letters they read made her admire him even more. Made her...*love him*...more strongly.

She'd gone to great pains to conceal the intensity of her emotions from him, save for the cheerful ones.

But there was no denying it. What she felt for Brent was love. No matter how much she tried to ignore her growing admiration, no matter how much she tried to focus solely on being Brent's friend, the affection she harbored for him continued to swell within her heart even as he continued to dash her hopes each day they spent together.

"I don't want you to get hurt," Jessie said.

"I know." Zoe twirled the whisk in her hand once more. "But that's a moot point now. And even though I know I shouldn't, I'm still harboring some small hope that he'll change his mind."

"If he doesn't, he's not worthy of you. You're the most wonderful person I've ever had the pleasure of knowing. And in the end, if he's truly not ready to let Kayla go, then you'll be better off in the long run to move on now."

Zoe flinched. "I'm afraid of how much I'll miss him if I let go of him altogether. Isn't being just friends with him better than nothing at all?"

"I don't know—that one's up to you. But if you do choose to let him go completely at some point, I'll be here for you. Every step of the way, until you're back on your feet, stronger than ever." Her tone firmed. "And you will be, Zoe. You're too tough to let a broken heart get you down for long."

Zoe closed her eyes and smiled. "You always know exactly what to say to make me feel better." She opened her eyes and laughed—a sincere one this time. One she savored as her best friend's comforting presence wrapped around her, cocooning her from the pain, helping her discover her cheery, Christmas-loving self again. "But don't think I don't know you're just trying to butter me up so that I'll bring you a batch of these frosted sugar cookies."

Jessie laughed, too. "I'll admit I want you to put my name at the top of the list for cookie delivery. And I'd just kill for some of those peppermint ones you made last year. The ones with the pink frosting? Are you and Miles whipping up a batch of those tonight?"

"Of course! Christmas just isn't Christmas without a dash of pink frosting."

A knock sounded at the door.

"He's here," Zoe said, picking up her phone. "I gotta go."

"Have fun frosting the cookies. And give Miles and Holly a kiss good-night for me, okay?"

"Will do." Zoe ended the call, shoved her phone into her back pocket and walked into the living room to answer the front door.

Miles, however, beat her to it, padding down the hall in his bare feet, dashing in front of her and yanking open the door. "It's frosting night, Mr. Brent!" He jumped up and down in his elf pajamas, his hair, still damp from the shower, sticking up in thick tufts around his ears. "And Zoe got a bunch of food coloring to make it pop. She got red, green, yellow, white, pink—"

"Miles." Zoe placed her hands on his shoulders, stilling his movements. "Let's not overwhelm Mr. Brent the moment he gets h—oof!"

Prince barreled into her legs, headbutting her thighs and yipping playfully.

Laughing, Zoe hugged him, then rubbed his furry head. "Look at you, mister! Always so eager to give me kisses!"

"Whoa there, buddy." Brent, his dark, windswept hair equally as adorable as Miles's, tugged Prince back by his collar and smiled. "I think he knew where I was headed and didn't want me to leave without him. Couldn't bring myself to leave him at home. I hope that's okay?"

"Of course." Grinning, she reached down and rubbed Prince's ears, then laughed again as Brent released his collar and Prince bounded into the kitchen, padded around the island and sat on the floor below where Holly sat in her rocker. "He's on guard duty again."

"Yep," Brent said. "And if I were this little man here—" he ruffled Miles's damp hair "—I'd be excited, too, at getting to frost cookies in elf pajamas." He winked, and that, coupled with his boyish grin, made Zoe's heart turn over in her chest. "I take it you're going to put me to work frosting cookies if I stay?"

Zoe narrowed her eyes up at him. "I take it that if you stay, you're going to make me work reading letters and coming up with a plan for a good deed?"

"Just one letter." He held up a long white business envelope. "But yes, that's the plan."

"All right." Zoe plucked the letter from his hand. "How 'bout you help Miles mix up some frosting while I read?"

Brent lowered to his haunches in front of Miles and held up his hand, palm out. "How about that, Miles? Think you and me can take charge of that frosting?"

"We sure can!" Smiling wide, Miles gave Brent a high-five, then grabbed his hand, tugged him back to his feet and led him through the living room to the kitchen.

Over the next few minutes, Zoe read the letter Brent had given her, pausing occasionally to give Brent and

Miles directions on how to mix the frosting, toss dirty utensils into the sink and retrieve a batch of freshly baked—but cooled—sugar cookies from a counter on the other side of the kitchen and place them on the island in front of Brent and Miles. And Prince remained well behaved, keeping a careful watch over Holly, licking her nose and wagging his tail affectionately at her every coo and playful gurgle.

"Oh, my." Finished reading, Zoe placed Emmett Lee's letter on the island, blinked away the moisture from her eyes and looked at Brent. "You're right. We have to help him."

A pleased—and somewhat proud—expression crossed Brent's face. "I knew you'd understand and would want to help."

"I do."

Prying her gaze away from the admiration in his eyes, she focused on the bowls of colorful icing arranged in a neat row on the island. Despite her misgivings about spending even more time with Brent, she couldn't ignore the fact that Emmett Lee was in pain and in need of comfort this Christmas season. Her mind returned to the letter she'd just read, turning over each of Emmett's pleading phrases in her mind, seeking a solution to the problem before them.

"He mentioned wanting kids around," she said, "and that he had a lot of Christmas stories to tell."

"I like Christmas stories!" Miles stood on the other side of the kitchen island, his mouth, chin and fingertips stained with multiple colors, as he jumped with excitement. "Maybe if we ask him, he'll tell me a few?"

Zoe grinned. "Possibly." She grabbed a napkin and wiped his face. "But you'll need to clean yourself up a good bit before you ask him. What did I tell you about eating the frosting? You keep this up and we'll have none left for the cookies."

Miles smiled, his teeth and tongue just as yellow as his fingertips. "Mr. Brent ate some, too. More than me!"

Brent held up his hands, his mouth twitching. "You'll find no icing on me. There's not a speck of yellow sugar on my skin."

Miles laughed. "That's because you ate it with a spoon instead of your hands."

Zoe sighed. "Well, if you're going to be a frosting thief, I suppose it's best that you have good manners when eating it as opposed to carrying around the yellow stain of guilt like Miles." She opened the drawer on the kitchen island, retrieved three plastic sandwich bags, then handed one to Brent and one to Miles. "Now fill each of those sandwich bags with one color of frosting, seal it, clip off one of the bag's bottom corners and start piping frosting onto these cookies while we strategize—*without eating it*."

Brent chuckled. "Yes, ma'am."

Doing her best not to focus on the tempting curve of his smile, Zoe scooped pink frosting into her own plastic bag, sealed it, clipped one end and began piping frosting onto the peppermint cookies she'd baked. "So let's see… Mr. Lee has a lot of Christmas stories he could tell and he'd like to have kids around for Christmas."

Brent looked thoughtful as he carefully piped red frosting onto a sugar cookie. "Maybe we could ask the parents of some of Miles's classmates if they'd be interested in asking their kids to sing some carols at Emmett's house and then maybe ask Mr. Lee to tell them some Christmas stories afterward?"

"I'd like that," Miles said. His tongue peeked out of the

corner of his mouth as he concentrated on piping green frosting onto a cookie instead of the counter. "And could we bring cookies, too? And fruit punch? Everyone in my class likes fruit punch."

Zoe stopped piping frosting, plopped the plastic bag onto the counter and smiled. "I've got it!" She ticked off ideas onto her fingertips. "Kids, Christmas stories and food. What better combination for a school Christmas party? You know, Kent Marsh, a seven-year-old boy that goes to the same elementary school as Miles, wrote to Santa a couple weeks ago and asked if he could trade his little sister for a big brother. I can't do anything about that, but he also asked for pizza, grape soda and candy bars at the school's Christmas party. So what if we gather up some pizza, grape soda, candy bars and all the extra fixings—" she smiled at Miles "—including cookies, and ask Mr. Lee if we can have the school Christmas party at his house?"

She pumped her fist in the air, the excitement at the prospect of filling Emmett's house with festive Christmas cheer making her almost as giddy as Miles.

"I've seen Mr. Lee's house," she continued. "It's a beautiful, three-story Victorian, and my hands are already itching to open up those boxes of Christmas decorations in his attic and put them to good use. I can call the elementary school principal in the morning—I've gotten to know her well since I enroll our foster children at the school so she won't mind me calling her on a Saturday—and clear the idea with her. If she agrees, we could stop by Mr. Lee's house after we collect letters from the Santa mailbox tomorrow afternoon and ask if he'd be willing to host. What do you think?"

Brent and Miles looked at each other and smiled.

Prince yipped, his mouth parting and tongue lolling out as if in a toothy grin. Even Holly who'd watched them, wide-eyed and silent, as they'd frosted cookies, wiggled in her rocker and cooed.

Brent reached over, slid his pointer finger into Holly's hand and smiled as her tiny fingers curled around his. "I'd say it's unanimous."

"So we're agreed, then." Zoe patted the plastic bag full of pink frosting in front of her. "After I get approval from the school principal and we check the Santa mailbox, we'll visit Mr. Lee." She glanced at the clock on the wall and winced. "But for now, someone—" she glanced at Miles, who was in the middle of yawning "—needs to wash off the frosting, brush his teeth, get in the bed and get a good night's sleep."

Miles stopped yawning and licked the last bit of frosting from his thumb. "Do I have to go to bed now? Mr. Brent's still here, and we could—"

"It's time for bed," Zoe said firmly. "We all need a good night's rest if we're going to tackle a new project tomorrow." She rounded the island, kissed the top of Miles's head, then nudged him toward the hallway. "Go wash off the frosting, brush your teeth and pick out a book. I'll be there soon to tuck you in and read you a story."

Miles grumbled under his breath but complied. He stopped halfway down the hall, glanced over his shoulder, then skipped back across the kitchen and threw his arms around Brent's waist. "Night, Mr. Brent." He hugged Brent tighter. "I'll see you tomorrow."

Brent smiled, his voice a bit husky as he hugged Miles back, his eyes meeting Zoe's. "Night, buddy."

She held his gaze for a moment, the sight of Miles in his strong, protective embrace—the very fact that Miles felt safe and secure enough to latch on to a male role model—evoking an almost overwhelming surge of affection.

"I-it's time for little girls to be in bed, too," Zoe said, kissing Holly's cheek. Holly cooed, but her eyes had grown heavy. "Say good-night to Mr. Brent, Holly." Zoe scooped the infant up into her arms and headed for the hallway, asking over her shoulder, "Brent, would you mind putting what's left of the frosting in the fridge? I'll take care of the dirty dishes after I get Holly settled."

Brent stood still as Miles released him, his eyes roving over Miles, then Holly and finally, Zoe. He cleared his throat, then said, "No problem. Take your time."

The gentle tenderness in his deep voice followed Zoe down the hall and lingered in her mind as she changed Holly's diaper, rocked her in the rocking chair of her nursery for a few minutes, then placed her in her crib. Her hands lingered on Holly's downy red hair, her mind playing different scenarios of Brent tucking Miles and Holly into bed. Brent, kneeling in the living room, petting Prince and whispering softly, settling the pup down for the night. Brent, meeting her eyes across the room, striding over and taking her hands in his. Telling her he'd made a mistake and that he'd changed his mind about their relation—

No! She squeezed her eyes shut and rubbed her temples, forcing the thought from her mind. *Don't go there. We're just friends. That's all.*

She could handle this—she had it under control.

When she returned to the kitchen, Brent was biting into a peppermint cookie.

"Hey!" Zoe laughed. "You're as bad as Miles—sneaking a sample every chance you get."

Brent, caught in the act, grinned. "My bad. But these

right here—" he held up the pink frosted cookie he'd bitten into "—are one of a kind." He took another bite, pausing as he chewed to say, "Gonna have to take a few of these for the road."

Oh, mercy! That charming grin and teasing tone… Zoe couldn't help but laugh with him. But when he grabbed another cookie, she crossed the kitchen and smacked his hand playfully. Prince barked, then padded off into the living room, sniffing the floor along the way.

"Not a chance, sir," she said, reaching for the cookie in Brent's hand. "Jessie already has first dibs on these, and we need to save a few to sweeten the deal with Mr. Lee tomorrow if we plan on getting him to agree to let us invade his house."

Chuckling, Brent set the cookie on the counter and caught her hand in his, his big palm cupping the back of hers, his strong fingers circling her wrist gently. "Your fingers are all pink."

Zoe looked down, the sight and feel of his strong, tanned hand supporting her own scattering her thoughts. "I-it's the food coloring."

Brent stared down at their hands, too, his smile fading. He examined her fingertips, stained with various colors of frosting, as they rested in his palm, wove his fingers between hers, then lifted his head and leaned toward her slightly, his attention lowering to her mouth.

She leaned in, too—the enticing thought of his lips gently touching hers almost impossible to resist.

He whispered in what sounded like a shocked tone, "You're so different."

From Kayla.

Zoe jerked away as the thought echoed in her mind.

That was what he'd meant. She was so different from

his late wife, the woman he'd told her he still loved—would always love.

And here she was, foolishly in love with him, eager for any scraps of affection he might throw her way.

Zoe tugged her hand from his grasp and spun away, covering her hot cheeks with clumsy hands, hiding the uncontrollable tremor in her chin. Oh, she'd lost so much dignity already. It was time to hold tight to what little remained.

The warmth of Brent's frame drew close at her back. His masculine scent surrounded her as he said urgently, "Zoe—"

"We've got a busy day tomorrow, and I have a lot to clean before I turn in for the night." Dignity. That was all she had left when it came to Brent Carson. "Will you see yourself out, please?"

Chapter Eight

Brent had messed up—big time!—in more ways than he could have anticipated.

The next afternoon, he stood dressed as Santa beside the Santa mailbox in Hope Springs's town square, facing a line of kids that seemed to stretch for miles while still kicking himself for being an inconsiderate jerk.

Zoe stood to his right, on the other side of the mailbox, cradling Holly close to her chest to block her tiny body against the cold. She smiled broadly at the kids who waited in line anxiously for their chance to drop their letter into the mailbox and meet Santa. Despite the recent plunge in temperature and blustery afternoon wind, Zoe had maintained a warm, welcoming disposition for every child who stepped up to the mailbox. She smiled when greeting parents, smiled at Holly when she bundled her more warmly in her arms and smiled down at Miles every few minutes, her pink stocking cap flopping against her long blond curls endearingly as she praised Miles for being a great elf. She even smiled at Prince, who sat at her feet guarding Holly, his antlers perched crookedly on his head.

Zoe had smiled her fantastic, engaging smile at everyone throughout the afternoon. Everyone except Brent. To him, she'd offered only two smiles: one polite smile when he'd picked up her, Miles and Holly at her cabin an hour earlier and one strained smile when she'd assumed her place beside him on the other side of the bright red mailbox to perform her duties as Santa's elf. To anyone else, nothing would seem amiss, but he'd grown accustomed to her carefree grins, enthusiastic laughter and teasing expressions...all of which he'd missed throughout the afternoon.

But her reserved interactions were to be expected, considering his behavior last night. He winced, recalling the firm dismissal she'd issued him in her cabin the night before.

Will you see yourself out, please?

Those terse words coming from Zoe had hurt him far more than he'd expected. Not once before then, in all the time he'd known her, had she asked him to leave her presence. Nor had she ever been the first to leave when she'd bumped into him in the coffee shop, on the hiking trails or in passing in town. He'd always been the first to walk away, keenly aware of her gaze following him as he left, with one exception—the morning she and Miles had visited his cabin the day Holly had been abandoned on his porch. He hadn't behaved well then, and he was afraid he'd behaved just as badly last night at Zoe's cabin.

He'd taken advantage of her.

Last night he'd touched her—really touched her—for the first time. Her hand, soft and delicate, had nestled perfectly within his larger one. The sensation of her pulse beneath the delicate skin of her wrist, fluttering against his thumb while he'd held her hand, had glowed inside him like warm coals on a blustery winter night, making him long to move close, gently touch his mouth to hers and simply savor the closeness of her presence.

Brent knew something had changed between the two of them. He'd felt the shift gradually over the past weeks, deep in his chest, where he'd hidden away the admiration he'd harbored for her for several years now. But while he'd always appreciated her, he knew that lately, his feelings for her had deepened. He'd grown eager to be in her presence, seeking opportunities to spend more time with her, talk with her and simply be near her.

He wanted to tell her…

Tell her what? Breath catching, he looked in her direction again, seeking her eyes, but she had lowered her head and was speaking softly to Holly, her long hair rippling over her shoulder, obscuring her face.

It was his own fault that she was standoffish around him now. He was the one who'd told her outright weeks ago that they should simply remain friends. At the time, he'd meant it.

But over the past weeks, he'd found himself wondering if only friendship with Zoe would be enough. Zoe, caring, compassionate and generous, had lingered on the fringes of his life for years and had slowly slipped into his heart recently, settling into it as though it had been fashioned just for her. He didn't want to just be friends with Zoe.

He loved her.

But that love still felt wrong somehow. Actually, his recent actions were what felt wrong at the moment. It was wrong to say he wanted to be just friends, and it had been wrong to confuse her about his feelings for her, however unintentionally, these past weeks.

What kind of man would do that? What kind of man could be so careless with a woman's heart?

"Hey, Santa!" A sharp pain ripped through Brent's right

shin just as a young boy asked impatiently, "Are you listening to me?"

Hissing in a breath, Brent rubbed his shin and looked down, eyeing what looked to be a six- or seven-year-old boy in front of him. The kid had brown hair, a large gap where one of his front teeth should've been and an irritated scowl on his face.

"You know, kid," Brent said, squatting down in front of the boy, "it's not nice to kick people—especially Santa."

The boy huffed out a breath. "Well, how else was I 'posed to get your attention? I would've pulled on your beard, but you're too tall. And it's fake anyway, right?"

Brent frowned. "Look, kid, I have a naughty list, you know?"

"Yeah, I know." The boy scowled. "I'm already on it. That's why I'm here."

A muffled giggle sounded beside Brent. He glanced up, catching a brief glimpse of Zoe's smile before she turned away again. There was also a teasing flash of compassion in her eyes as her gaze had momentarily met his. Finally! A small sign that she might be inclined to forgive him for his insensitive behavior last night.

"See, the thing is," the boy continued, "I want to know how I can get off the bad list. I ain't got but a few more days till Christmas, so I'm not sure there's anything I can do, but I thought I'd ask just the same."

Brent stroked his fake beard thoughtfully, then said, "The best way to make up for the bad things you've done is to do good things. You have, as you said, a few more days until Christmas. My advice is to do as many good deeds as you can between now and then."

The boy mulled this over, his brow wrinkling as he

studied Brent's expression. "Do I have to do something good for my sister, too?"

"Yes. That would be best." Brent patted his big belly, courtesy of the pillow he'd stuffed beneath his Santa jacket, and deepened his voice. "And apologize to everyone you've wronged. Those two things would be a great place to start."

The boy shrugged, then walked away, glancing back after a few steps to say, "Sorry about kicking you, Santa. Does that apology count toward gettin' off the bad list?"

Brent nodded ruefully. "I suppose so." He rubbed his injured shin once more as the boy left, then glanced at Zoe. "And you want me to pose for pictures with kids like that?"

"Children like him are still growing and learning. Today you helped him learn two ways he can be a better person to those around him. That alone is worth you dressing up and being here." Zoe lifted one eyebrow and tilted her head. "Besides, you posing for pictures with the kids was the only request the PTA at the elementary school had. They agreed to move the school's Christmas party to Mr. Lee's house—provided he approves, of course—as long as we perform as Santa and Mrs. Claus for pictures with the kids at the Christmas play reception." She shrugged. "In the end, we'll end up doing a good deed for Mr. Lee as well as the school. It's a win-win."

A low growl rumbled up Brent's chest and escaped his mouth even as his lips quirked into a grin. Here he was at odds again, dreading the idea of being stuffed into a hot Santa suit for an hour-long photo session at the school but excited at the thought of contributing to Miles's school's Christmas celebration. Doing another good deed dressed as Santa—no matter how much the fake beard made his chin itch—meant seeing kids smile, giggle and jump in place with anticipation of telling him their Christmas wishes. It also meant having Zoe stand by his side, dressed as Mrs. Claus, welcoming each child who sought a photo with Santa.

Having the opportunity to spend time in close proximity with Zoe again made it all worthwhile. And the thought of celebrating the holidays leading up to Christmas Day rather than spending them alone in his cabin as he had done in previous years sparked an unexpected joy in his heart.

"I've got your number."

Brent glanced at Zoe when she spoke, the sincere grin of affection spreading across her face as she looked up at him making him catch his breath.

"You act like you don't enjoy being Santa," she continued. "But deep down, I think you do. And I think you're actually beginning to enjoy celebrating the season."

He held her gaze, unable to look away or ignore the images forming in his mind. Images of spending future Christmas holidays with Zoe, Miles and maybe even baby Holly, putting up pink Christmas trees, performing good deeds for neighbors and greeting each new morning with eager anticipation of all the good things God would bring. It sounded a whole lot more fulfilling than remaining submerged beneath a deep sludge of grief, dwelling on what he'd lost.

"Yes," he whispered. "I am enjoying it. Every moment."

Her smile dimmed. She shook her head slightly, then glanced down as the last child in line stepped forward. The girl dropped her letter into the Santa mailbox and smiled up at Brent before waving goodbye as she skipped back to her parents.

"That's the last of them." Zoe walked around the mailbox to Brent's side and nodded toward Holly, who rested comfortably in her arms. "Would you mind holding Holly? Miles and I will load the letters in the Santa bag, take it to the truck and I'll grab Holly's stroller so we can make our way over to Mr. Lee's house." She pointed across the town square at a small cluster of large houses that lined the sidewalk. "It's only a couple blocks that way. We'll walk over, pitch our idea and be home well before dark."

"Sounds good to me." Brent cradled Holly to his chest gently as Zoe transferred her into his arms. "The sooner I can get this beard off, the better. It's itching like crazy."

Zoe laughed, that glow of joy returning to her face, brightening her expression. "When it gets really bad, just think of how I'll feel wearing a wool skirt, gray wig and spectacles."

Brent chuckled, watching as Zoe and Miles opened the back of the Santa mailbox and moved the letters into the large, red bag Miles held. He could imagine Zoe as Mrs. Claus very easily. How adorable she'd look dressed as Santa's bubbly wife and how much Christmas cheer she'd bring to each child she would greet at the Christmas play reception. And he found himself imagining so much more—

"We've only emptied the mailbox halfway, and the bag's already full," Zoe said, slinging the bag they'd filled with letters over her shoulder. "We'll load this bag in the truck and get the rest of the letters Monday. Come on, guys."

Brent watched Zoe lead Miles and Prince across the town square to his truck. The way Zoe held Miles's hand and spoke praises to Prince, who still wore his reindeer antlers as he padded across the dormant grass after her, brought a smile to his face.

He looked down at Holly, who looked back up at him with her wide blue eyes, blinking slowly. The warm weight of her in his arms was just as comforting as it had been the first time that he'd held her in Zoe's cabin.

"Hey, gorgeous," he whispered, drifting the back of his finger along her soft cheek. "It's a good thing you landed in Zoe's arms. She's a wonderful mom, and she'll make sure there's a wonderful future waiting for you."

A future filled with joyful Christmases, festive birthdays and sunny summers. A safe, secure home to experience her first steps and a welcoming community to embrace her on her first day of school. There were so many beautiful moments for Holly to look forward to over the coming years. Ones he found himself wishing that he could be a part of with Zoe and Miles…maybe as a family?

His heart swelled at the prospect of being a husband and father again, of having Zoe by his side and Miles and Holly to nurture, protect and guide through life.

Holly cooed up at him, one tiny fist slipping free of the warm blanket Zoe had bundled her in, her hand opening and closing, grasping at air.

Brent slid his pinky finger against her palm and smiled as she latched on, a sheen of moisture coating his eyes as he whispered, "You started all of this." He bent his head and kissed her warm cheek. "How glad I am that you came to my door."

"Thank you."

Brent looked up with surprise. A young woman who looked to be in her late teens or early twenties stood before him, bundled up in a long red jacket, thick scarf and wool hat. Her clothes seemed too large for her, cloaking her small form, and her wool hat hid her hair, highlighting her eyes which stared up at him below the cuffed brim.

Brent's attention lingered on her eyes, noting the intensity in their blue depths. "For what?"

She didn't answer. Instead she looked at Holly, a bittersweet smile crossing her face as she studied the infant in silence. After a moment, she walked over to the mailbox, opened the front latch, dropped in a letter, then walked away.

Cradling Holly closer to him, Brent watched the woman leave, scrutinizing her gait, searching for a glimpse of red hair. "Wait! Are you...?"

The young woman glanced over her shoulder, a bright smile on her face as she continued walking away, "You're the best, Santa!"

"Are you sure you didn't recognize her?" Zoe huddled closer to Brent's side as she pushed Holly's stroller down the sidewalk toward Emmett Lee's house. "Was she wearing a white jacket? Did she have red hair? Did she walk the same way? Did you recognize her voi—"

"I honestly don't know, Zoe." Sighing, Brent reached down into the stroller and tucked the thick blanket more snugly around Holly, keeping her warm against the winter wind. "She didn't have on a white jacket, and she was wearing a wool hat that covered her hair, so I couldn't see what color it was. And during the one brief glimpse I had of Holly's mom, she was running away from me through the woods. I didn't see her face or hear her voice, and short of her being in the exact same white coat with her hair down, I doubt I'd be able to recognize her." He frowned. "Though..."

His voice drifted off as he looked ahead, his dark eyes

scanning the large houses they passed as they walked along the sidewalk.

"Though what?" Leaning closer, Zoe nudged him with her elbow. "Go ahead. What were you going to say?"

His brow creased. "She acted as though she knew who I was underneath the Santa outfit. And there was something in her tone. I can't put my finger on it, but it was the way she spoke, the way she looked Holly." He moved his strong hands in the air as though searching for the right words. "And she had these really blue eyes like—"

"Like Holly's?" Zoe's heart kicked against her ribs, both excitement and dread whirling inside her stomach at the thought of having potentially found Holly's mother. "What is your gut telling you? Do you feel like it was the same woman who brought Holly to your house? Do you think she was Holly's mother?"

Zoe held her breath, the sound of her shoes scraping across the sidewalk filling the silence as Brent considered this. She knew what answer she should be hoping for. That she should pray with every bit of hope in her heart that the woman who'd approached Brent at the Santa mailbox minutes earlier had been Holly's mother. That perhaps the young woman had changed her mind about abandoning her daughter and had decided to seek her out again and possibly reclaim her.

Wouldn't that be what a good foster mother would want for the orphaned child she was caring for? Wasn't the ideal outcome of situations such as this that the child be reunited with her biological mother? That Holly would end up safe, loved and supported by the mother who'd given birth to her and who shared her blood?

Zoe gripped the handle of Holly's stroller tighter, her mind balking at the desperate longing that still bloomed in her heart despite her rationalizations. She hadn't even had Holly for a month. She shouldn't feel such a strong attachment to the infant, shouldn't be terrified at the thought of letting Holly go and shouldn't feel as though she were Holly's...*mother.*

"I don't know," Brent said. "But if it was her, she looked happy to see Holly with me. Even...relieved, I'd go so far to say. Though she didn't look surprised to see me holding Holly. So if that really was Holly's mother, she must've already seen us here with Holly on one of the other days we've been here and since she didn't mention it, she obviously doesn't want to be found."

"But what about the letter? Didn't you say she left a letter?"

"Yeah, but she didn't hand it directly to me. She dropped it in the mailbox with the others, which means it'll take a lot of sifting, reading and analyzing to figure out which one was hers. Anyway, if what she wrote pertained to getting Holly back, I think she would've given it directly to me—or taken it to Hummingbird Haven."

Zoe released a deep breath, her nerves calming. "Jessie and I have searched every town nearby and spoken to every contact we have, and we still haven't found anyone who could potentially be related to Holly or know anything about her abandonment." She bit her lip and looked up at Brent, speaking earnestly. "Maybe...maybe not locating her isn't a bad thing. Maybe God wants Holly to be with me."

"Maybe." Brent ducked his head and leaned closer, his broad chest blocking the wind as it whipped against her cheek and neck. "But two little ears have perked up and are straining to hear every word we're saying right now, so we may want to save this conversation for later."

She glanced ahead, where Miles strolled in front of them along the sidewalk, holding Prince's leash as the pup trotted close to his side. Miles's head was tilted in their direction, a curious expression on his face.

"Yeah," she said. "You're right. I think it's best we save this conversation for later."

The last thing she wanted to do was entangle Miles in the search for Holly's mother. Miles had only just begun to recover from his own mother's abandonment, and he'd grown as close to Holly as she had over these past few weeks. The three of them—her, Miles and Holly—had fallen into a comfortable rhythm over the days they'd spent in each other's company, enjoying breakfast together first thing every morning, settling down in the living room together after Miles returned from school each day to hear how his day went and help him with his homework and setting up a nursery in the spare room for Holly. Miles had even taken to singing to Holly in the evening, patting her back gently and kissing her forehead as he wished her good-night.

They'd grown to feel like their own little family, especially since Brent had begun spending so much time with them. Even now, if she allowed her mind to drift and suspended reality for a few brief moments, she could easily envision herself as Holly and Miles's mother, who was enjoying a stroll down a sidewalk in the heart of Hope Springs with the man she loved by her side.

A wave of pain rolled through Zoe, reminding her how dangerous that thought could be to an already heavily damaged heart.

"Is that it?" Brent pointed at a large house to their left, five feet ahead.

Zoe smiled, her troubled thoughts dissipating. "Oh, yes. That's the one."

It was hard to miss. Right there, amid modern homes fashioned with siding and clean lines, stood a Victorian beauty, boasting a pitched roof, wraparound porch and cylindrical turrets. The white two-story home with intricate woodwork and ornate details was picture-perfect for the Christmas season.

Zoe tilted her head back as they approached, studying the vintage wall lanterns adorning each side of the double-doored entrance, decorative woodwork along the railing and stained glass windows embedded within each of the two wooden front doors.

"It's huge!" Miles bounded ahead of them with Prince nipping at his heels, skipping up the front steps, standing on the porch and spreading his arms wide as he smiled up at the steep, gabled roofs.

"Yep." Brent studied the house in front of them, his mouth curving into a smile. "It's magnificent."

"It's perfect." A rush of Christmas cheer lifted Zoe's spirits into a giddy high. Her hand automatically sought Brent's larger one, curling around it, squeezing it tightly and tugging him along with her to the front steps as she carefully navigated Holly's stroller along the paved path toward the house. "Oh, I hope he's home and I hope he agrees. Can you imagine how beautiful this house will look decked out with the Christmas decorations in Mr. Lee's attic? What kind of decorations do you think we'll find boxed up in there? From the sound of his letter, he and his late wife adored this house, and I'd imagine they took great care to pick out decorations that would pair perfectly with a Victorian home. I'm thinking thick evergreen garlands, big silky bows, candlelit lanterns, flocked pine-cones, lots of red berries and, of course, tons of holly—"

"Whoa, there." Brent tugged her to a stop at the bottom step of the front porch, then unbuckled Holly and lifted her, wrapped in a warm blanket, into his arms. "We're as excited as you are, aren't we, Holly?" He glanced up, smiling. "But we have to get him to say yes first, don't we? I mean, at least before we go poking around in his attic."

The teasing charm in his dark eyes and handsome smile sent delicious shivers up Zoe's spine. "Yes." She dragged her shaky hands over the pants of her elf costume and strived for a calm disposition. "You're absolutely right. I need to appeal to Mr. Lee's goodwill politely and calmly. And if he says no…"

Brent raised one eyebrow.

"I'll either bribe him with a million peppermint cookies or guilt-trip him by reminding him of how many little children's hearts he'll break."

Brent's chuckle followed her as she walked up the front steps. "Don't forget we're doing this as a good deed for him—not us."

"Of course!" Zoe joined Miles at the front door where Prince had laid down, sprawling his tired legs and paws across the front porch, and rang the doorbell. "But it sure wouldn't be a hardship for us to enjoy having the Christmas party here as well, now, would it?"

Miles beamed up at her with excitement. "It sure wouldn't!"

Boards creaked, footsteps shuffled, then the door opened and Mr. Lee, a tall man with gray hair and kind—but sad—eyes greeted them.

"What a nice surprise!" Leaning on a wooden cane for support, his drawn expression lit up as he looked down at

Miles, Zoe and Prince. "I don't think I've ever had elves and a reindeer call around here before."

Miles laughed. "Yes, sir. We're special elves with an invitation."

Mr. Lee laughed, too, his eyes leaving them and focusing on Brent who stood behind them, cradling Holly to his chest. "And Santa's here, too." The pleased excitement in his expression faded just a bit. "I take it you received my letter, Santa."

Brent eased closer, holding Holly securely with one arm and extending the other. "Yes, sir. And we'd truly appreciate it if you could forgive us for barging in on you. Could you possibly spare us a few minutes of your time?"

Mr. Lee shook his hand and his smile returned. "My mama taught me to never turn a stranger away—especially at Christmas." He stepped back, his cane tapping across the hardwood floor, and waved an arm toward the interior of the house. "Please come in. Looks like your pup's happy enough out here. I'll fix him up a bowl of water while you make yourselves comfortable in the sitting room just to your left there."

Zoe looped Prince's leash around the leg of one of the sturdy wicker chairs on the front porch, then the rest of them followed Mr. Lee inside, strolling carefully across the hardwood floors, gazing up at the high ceilings, admiring the ornate staircase and intricate wooden trim throughout each room and finally, settling onto a wide couch with plush cushions in the sitting room Emmett had directed them to.

After placing a bowl of water on the front porch for Prince, Mr. Lee walked slowly into the sitting room and eased into a chair across from them with a groan, taking a few moments to catch his breath. His hazel eyes roved over them slowly, the deep crow's feet fanning out at the edges of his eyelids and dark circles beneath his lower lashes lending him a solemn, heavy air.

"I'd offer you folks a cup of coffee and a treat for the little one—" he smiled down at Miles, then Holly, who still lay quietly in Brent's arms, her wide gaze taking in her new surroundings "—but I have nothing prepared to entertain guests, seeing as how I don't get many around here."

Zoe smiled gently, the gloomy tone of his voice making her heart ache. "Thank you, Mr. Lee, but we don't want to put you to any more trouble."

"Emmett, please."

She nodded. "Emmett. I'm Zoe Price. I think we've met once or twice before." At his nod, she continued, "And this is Miles and Holly and—"

"Santa." Emmett narrowed his eyes at Brent, his mouth pursing. "Also known as Brent Carson, tour guide extraordinaire. You're well known around these parts. I've heard a lot about both you and Ms. Price here, though we haven't been formally introduced." He smiled. "But where's your beard, Santa?"

Brent, seated beside Zoe, chuckled, the deep rumble vibrating his muscular arm against hers. "It gets a bit itchy now and then. I took a chance that you wouldn't mind if I came clean-shaven."

"Not at all. I'm glad you folks stopped by." Emmett looked down at his worn house shoes and tapped his cane against the floor. "I want to apologize to you. I was down the day I wrote to you. Got a bit maudlin." He glanced up, his hollowed cheeks flushing. "I'm sorry to have bothered you with my complaints. I'm not usually so pessimistic, but as I said, it was a tough day."

"Oh, no." Brent shook his head. "Please don't feel you

need to apologize. We're glad you wrote to us. As a matter of fact, we're here to ask a favor of you." He glanced at Zoe and lifted his chin. "Would you like to explain?"

Nodding, Zoe cleared her throat, scooted to the edge of the couch and folded her hands together in her lap. "You have a beautiful home, Emmett. Even more beautiful than you alluded to in your letter. And when you expressed a desire to see it filled with kids and graced with your Christmas decorations again, well, we got to thinking that a change of setting may be good for the annual elementary school Christmas party, and that your house would be the perfect new site to host the party. That is, if you'd be willing to let us invade your home and raid the Christmas decorations in your attic?"

A slow smile lifted Emmett's cheeks. "A Christmas party? Here?" He rubbed his grizzled chin. "That sounds delightful." He patted his thigh with his gnarled fingers. "But I—I have to be honest with you. I have arthritis and I have a lot of trouble getting around as of late, so I don't know that I'd be of much help—"

"But your stories!" Miles stood up and walked over to Emmett's chair. "In your letter, you said you have a lot of Christmas stories—and pictures! You have so many pictures, and there's probably a story for each one." He picked up a small picture frame from a small side table beside Emmett's chair and smiled. "Like this lady here that's decorating a Christmas tree. Who's she?"

Zoe blushed. "Miles, please don't—"

"He's okay." Smiling, Emmett took the framed picture from Miles and tapped it with one finger. "This is my wife, Constance. And this was the tree we had for Christmas during the first year we lived in this house." His expression and tone softened as though he were relishing a nostalgic memory. "Oh, but it was a big 'un. We chopped it down ourselves in the woods and hauled it back down here. It was an eight-footer. Took forever to get it in the house and set it up. But once we did, it sure was a sight to behold."

"My wife and I did that, too."

Zoe stilled. The bittersweet tone in Brent's voice renewed a painful ache deep inside her that she tried to ignore.

"We'd hike in the woods behind my cabin," Brent continued, "cut down a tree and bring it back." His voice changed, deepening with sorrow, and Zoe couldn't bring herself to look at him. "I lost her six years ago."

"What was her name?" Emmett asked.

"Kayla." Brent laughed, the warm tone returning to his voice. "She's the one who always took charge of decorating our tree every year. Red bows and gold ornaments—the traditional look all the way."

Zoe cringed. Oh, gracious. Her pink tree with white-and-silver decorations must have seemed garish to Brent in light of the traditionally decorated tree he'd had with his wife.

Emmett laughed, too. "Constance was exactly the same. She was very particular about our Christmas decor. Always had me position the gold star on the top of the tree just right. And when we finished, we'd have cocoa and—"

"Tell stories?" Miles eased closer and placed his hand on Emmett's arm. "Did you and Mrs. Constance talk about Christmas stories of when you grew up here?"

Emmett smiled wide. "Boy, did we ever—though I'd call them memories more than stories. She grew up around here, too. Had as many memories—or stories—to tell as I did."

"Miles loves Christmas stories." Zoe forced a cheery smile to her face. "He was hoping you'd be willing to tell him and his classmates stories about the Christmases you enjoyed in Hope Springs as a kid. They have story time at the Christmas party every year and it would be a perfect time for you to share your fondest memories. You wouldn't have to lift a finger, otherwise. Brent and I, along with the school's PTA and some of the parents, will handle putting up all of your Christmas decorations and preparing the food."

Emmett smiled at Miles and patted his cheek. "Then I'd be happy—and honored—to host your Christmas party, young Miles."

Miles squealed, jumped up and down and threw his arms around Emmett's shoulders in a bear hug. "Thank you, Mr. Lee! Everyone's gonna love having the Christmas party here!"

Emmett hugged Miles back, his entire expression brightening. "I'm looking forward to it already. When's the date, Zoe?"

"Very soon," she said. "The school's Christmas play is this Tuesday night—we'd love for you to come, by the way!—and that happens to be the last day of school before Christmas break. The school's Christmas party will be held the day after that, just after dark, so the Christmas lights will be bright and give the best atmosphere for the party. We'll need to bring the boxes down from the attic and start decorating right away, if that's okay with you?"

Emmett nodded and returned the framed picture back to the side table. "I have one request, if it's not too much trouble?"

Zoe shook her head. "After you graciously allowed us

to have the party in your gorgeous home? Nothing you asked for would be too much, Emmett."

"There's a special candle in my attic, along with the rest of the Christmas decorations. It's a large one, with a brass handle attached. Every year, I put it in the front window to remember Constance. It's a tradition I've celebrated for ten years now." He looked at Brent, a sympathetic gleam in his eyes. "There's one more like it up there as well. Perhaps we could put that candle out for your wife, Kayla? That way the women we love will be with us in spirit even though they can't be with us in person."

Zoe froze, struggling to maintain a polite smile, as Brent answered softly, "I'd love that."

Chapter Nine

❧

The following Tuesday, Zoe, getting dressed as Mrs. Claus for the Christmas play, was rewarded with an unexpectedly pleasant glimpse into her future.

"Hm, how 'bout that?" Zoe adjusted the small spectacles on the bridge of her nose as she surveyed her reflection in a full-length mirror in her bedroom. "Pearl-gray hair rather suits me, and I think these glasses make me look a great deal wiser." She glanced over her shoulder at the bed where Miles sat, dangling his legs, beside Holly, who wiggled on her back and cooed up at the ceiling. "Whatcha think, little dude? Do I look shrewd or what?"

Miles rubbed his nose and giggled. "What's *shooed* mean?"

"Shrewd. *S-h-r-e-w-d*." Zoe fluffed the short gray curls of the wig and the faux-fur collar and cuffs she wore. The velvet costume, complete with frilly apron and shiny black dress boots, was surprisingly comfortable. "It means smart. Or having a way with people and situations to turn them to your advantage."

"Okay." Miles adjusted the collar of his elf costume. "I think you look like that. But I think you look like something else, too."

Smiling, Zoe crossed the bedroom and knelt in front

of him by the bed. "Oh, yeah? What is it that I look like? Mrs. Claus, maybe?"

"Yeah, but…" Miles reached out and gently twirled one of her gray curls around his finger. "You look like a pretty grandma, too."

"Really?" Zoe wrinkled her nose. "But what if I don't prefer the term *grandma*?" She tapped her chin thoughtfully. "What if I preferred the term *nana*? Or *gammie*? Or—" she tickled his ribs "—the grandest grand-foster-mother who ever walked the earth?"

Miles doubled over, giggling. "It—it doesn't matter. Whatever you call yourself, you'll still be pretty."

"Are you sure about that?" She tickled him a little more, enjoying the joyful, carefree sound of his laughter. "What if I don't age as well as you think? What if, as I grow older, I get warts on my nose, talons on my toes and sprout a lizard tail?"

"Won't matter!" Miles's laughter eased as she stopped tickling him. "I know you'll be pretty because I think all grandmas are pretty. And you'll be the most pretty grandma of all of 'em."

Zoe smiled. "And why's that?"

"Because grandmas always take care of you and love you no matter what. And you're already like that now." He grinned up at her. "You take care of me and Holly and love us no matter what."

The admiration in his big brown eyes and tender tone in his voice made her knees buckle, and she sank back onto her heels. "Sweet, sweet Miles." She reached up and smoothed a wayward strand of hair from his forehead. "What a good heart you have."

Miles's brows rose. "Good enough to get my Christmas wish?"

Zoe tapped his nose. "I think you've been so good this year that Santa will bring you whatever your heart desires."

Miles's expression lit up with excitement. He tugged a folded envelope from his pocket and placed it in Zoe's hand. "Then will you give this to him? To the real Santa, I mean? Not Mr. Brent." He tilted his head, a somber look in his eyes. "I know Mr. Brent only pretends to be Santa for the Santa mailbox and that he answers those letters on account that the real Santa's so busy and all. But you have a way to get in touch with the real Santa, don't you?"

Zoe nodded, offering up a silent prayer of thanks that Miles's innocent belief in the joy of Santa Claus remained intact. "I sure do."

Miles scooted to the edge of the bed. "Then will you give him my letter? And will you read it, please? Just to see if it sounds okay before you send it? I worked real hard on it."

"I'd be honored." Zoe slid her legs from beneath her, plopped onto her bottom and opened the envelope. Huddling closer to Miles with a giddy shiver of holiday excitement, she withdrew the letter and began reading.

Deer Santa

I now u are very bisee and dont have much time. But if it is not 2 much trouble will you please ask God 2 give me something? 2 things maybe?

I want 2 do good in my Christmas play at school. I want 2 make Zoe and Mr Brent pride of me. I want 2 remember what I shud say in the play.

My number 2. My mom left me and no 1 can find Holly's mom. So can me and Holly stay with Zoe? She is a good mom. I love her. She loves us 2.

I want to stay with Zoe forever and ever. I want

Holly to bee my sistur. I want us 2 be a famlee. Can Mr Brent be a part 2 of the famlee? He is fun. And nice now. I think he would be a good dad 2 half.

Thank you for the presants u give every 1 and the fun and the good stuff.
Love Miles

Zoe sat silently for a moment, cradling the letter between her palms, blinking back tears and trying to find her voice. "I... This is a beautiful letter, Miles." She glanced up, smiling at the deep blush staining Miles's cheeks. "And you know what?"

Miles bit his lip, then whispered. "What?"

"I love you, too." Zoe rose to her knees again, wrapped her arms around Miles and hugged him close. "Very much. More than I thought I could ever love someone. I'm so happy you came to live with me."

He wrapped his arms around her neck, his little hands clinging to her shoulders. "And Holly, too?"

She cupped the back of his head and sifted her fingers through his soft hair, breathing him in. "Yes. Holly, too."

"And will you let us stay with you? Will you be our mom? Forever?"

She squeezed him gently once more, then eased back and tipped up his chin with one finger, bringing his gaze to hers. "I want that more than anything in the world."

Miles smiled and twirled one of her gray curls around his finger again. "So you think Santa will ask God to make it happen?"

"I think he'll do his very best."

"And do you think God'll let Mr. Brent be me and Holly's dad?" His hands stilled in her hair, a hesitant look in his eyes as he looked up at her. "I know he wasn't very nice at first, but now I like him a lot. And he does nice things for other people, like you do. It'd be fun if he came to live with us. I think he'd be a good dad, don't you?"

Zoe's stomach plummeted, sinking deep within her, weighing her down against the floor. "I—I think Mr. Brent would be a very good father. But..." She took his hands in hers, trying to still the tremors in her voice. "But Mr. Brent is just our friend. He has his own home and his own life, and I think he's happy with things the way they are."

"I know." Hope vibrated in his tone. "But that could change, couldn't it? He might want to be my dad. Maybe if I ask him, he'll say yes?"

Oh, gracious. She had no idea what to say. So far, she hadn't been able to solve the dilemma of her own unrequited love for Brent. She'd been unable to let Brent go even though being just his friend had been excruciatingly painful to her heart.

Of course, she'd noticed Miles and Brent growing closer over the past weeks. She could tell from the smiles on their faces, the jovial tone in their voices when Brent chatted with Miles during their visits to the Santa mailbox, the times they spent sipping cocoa, opening letters and reading them in her cabin. She'd even noticed a serene—almost wishful—gleam in Brent's eyes during the times he'd held Holly protectively against his chest. And she'd especially noticed how much fun Miles and Brent had had over the past few days decorating Emmett's house for the school's Christmas party and frosting dozens and dozens of cookies back at Zoe's cabin in preparation for the big party night.

But she also knew exactly how far and fast Brent would run if Miles even hinted at the idea of wanting him for a dad. Brent's heart—his love and loyalty—were devoted to the wife and little girl he'd lost years ago. Brent had told her as much himself weeks ago, the day she'd helped him scout out a tree for Riley Jenkins behind his cabin.

Only, how could she explain it? How could she tell Miles the truth without—

No! Allowing Brent to break her heart was one thing, but allowing him to break Miles's heart, however unintentionally, was not something she could tolerate. Brent was a good man—she wouldn't have fallen in love with him otherwise—but loving him had become a painful experience for her. An experience she'd do her best to protect Miles from enduring.

But…the solution to healing her broken heart and protecting Miles's heart had been there all along. It rang clear as a Christmas bell once she managed to summon enough courage to face it.

"Do you remember the talk we had when you first came to live with me?" she asked Miles softly. "When you asked me why your mom left and hadn't come back?"

His expression dimmed. "Kind of."

"We talked about how God has a reason for everything. That He has a way of working things out for the best, even if we don't understand it, remember?"

He nodded.

"I still believe that," she whispered. "It's difficult at times—especially when I want something so badly that doesn't seem to be in God's plan. When I think having a certain thing might make me happy but God won't give it to me, I have a really difficult time trusting that He knows best. And sometimes I think that if I just work hard enough, I can make what I want happen. That maybe if I can show Him that this one thing is what I need that eventually He'll agree with me and allow it to happen." Her mouth shook and she bit her lip. "It hurts when you want something so much but can't have it. But in the end, I truly believe that God works everything out for the best, even if what happens is not exactly what we want at the time. He sees and knows things we don't, and sometimes letting go of what you want and waiting for God to send you what He knows is really best for you is the better thing to do."

Miles looked down and turned his hands over in her palms, his fingers drawing circles on her wrist. "So, I shouldn't ask Mr. Brent to be my dad?"

Zoe moved closer and squeezed his hands. "What I mean is that I think we should let God do the work. We can hope, we can dream and we can look forward to God bringing us the good things that He knows are best for us. And maybe one day, when He feels the time is right, He'll send a good man to be your father. But for now, I'm dreaming the same dream as you—that you, Holly and I might be a real family, in every sense of the word, one day soon. Because I can't imagine my life without either of you in it."

He lifted his head. "And the three of us being a family might be one of the good things God brings?"

Zoe nodded. "I'm praying real, real hard for that."

Miles's smile returned. He released one of her hands and reached over, holding one of Holly's hands in his own as she lay on the bed, kicking her bare feet and babbling softly beside them. "Then me and Holly will pray for that, too."

Zoe kissed his forehead and hugged him once more. "Now, in the meantime, why don't you go slip on your shoes and elf hat while I finish getting Holly ready so that we'll be ready to go when Mr. Brent picks us up in a few minutes?" She winked and tapped his chin. "I know you're going to do a wonderful job in this play tonight, but I'll be proud of you whether you make a mistake or not."

"Thanks, Zoe." Miles sprang off the couch, ran across the bedroom and into the hall, saying over his shoulder, "I'm going to be the best elf ever! You just wait and see!"

Zoe sat on the edge of the bed beside Holly, slipped her pinky into the infant's grasping hand and listened to the sound of Miles's footsteps running down the hall toward his room.

Closing her eyes, she thought of the future. She thought of adopting Miles and, hopefully, Holly, too. She calculated how long it might take to complete the process to officially transition from their foster mother to their permanent guardian and envisioned how fulfilling that life would be, how exciting, challenging and rewarding her days would become once she was legally named Miles and Holly's mother. And she tried to prepare for the other task that lay before her. One she needed to complete as soon as possible.

It was too painful—and dangerous for the well-being of Miles's heart—to continue welcoming Brent into her life so frequently. She'd done the good deed she had set out to do. She'd helped Brent heal and find joy during the holidays. And now it was time to let him go.

For Miles's sake…and her own.

"It's your turn, Amelia. Tell Santa what you want for Christmas."

Brent, dressed as Santa and seated in a decorative red chair in the auditorium of Hope Springs Elementary School, smiled at the mother and little girl with red pigtails who stood in front of him. "Merry Christmas, Amelia. Would you like to tell me your Christmas wish?"

Amelia looked up at him and grinned, lifting her hand toward his beard. "Is that real?"

Brent chuckled. "What do you think?"

Throughout the hour he'd spent greeting the long line of children who waited in the auditorium to speak to Santa and take a holiday picture before the school's Christmas play, he'd been asked that same question more than a dozen times. And each time, the child who asked the question had the same subsequent request.

"Can I test it, please?" Amelia asked.

Brent leaned forward and braced himself. "Be my guest."

Amelia had a strong grip for such a little girl, but he was prepared—he'd tied an extra knot in the elastic strap that secured the fake beard to his jaw, and the white locks barely moved when she yanked.

Seemingly satisfied, she smiled and patted his knee. "Is it okay if I sit here?"

"Sure thing." Brent waited as she climbed up onto one of his knees, looked over her shoulder and smiled at her mother who stood several feet away.

"Should I tell him what I want now, Mama?" Amelia asked.

Amelia's mother smiled encouragingly. "Go ahead, sweetheart."

Amelia faced him again, leaned close and whispered in his ear, "I'm okay with whatever you want to bring me. I've been very good this year, so I'm pretty sure you're going to bring me something. But if I have a choice about what you bring me, would you bring me a new baby doll, please? One with red hair like me?" She turned to the left of him where Zoe, dressed as Mrs. Claus, stood cradling

Holly against her chest, and pointed at Holly's red hair. "And like Mrs. Claus's baby?"

Brent glanced up, meeting Zoe's eyes as she smiled. He stifled a laugh at the amused joy in her expression, still surprised by how beautiful she looked dressed in a frilly red dress, gray wig and tiny glasses. Even with her blond hair hidden by her wig and her pretty features somewhat obscured by the thick curls and glasses, the kind gleam in her eye and bright smile still shone through. And those were a welcome sight, considering she'd seemed so distant when he'd picked up her, Miles and Holly earlier.

When he'd arrived at her cabin to escort them to the play, he'd expected her to bound out with Miles and Holly, hustle to the truck and hop into the front seat, vibrating with holiday cheer. That was, he had discovered over the past few weeks, her usual mood when they checked the Santa mailbox, performed a good holiday deed or attended a special holiday event.

But tonight had started out differently. She'd smiled when she'd slid into the passenger seat of his truck's cab and greeted him as usual, but her tone had been cooler than normal—reserved, even—and during the drive to the elementary school, she'd responded to his attempts at conversation politely but hadn't initiated any of her own.

Miles, excited and nervous about his impending performance in the school's Christmas play, had filled the truck with his chatter instead. And though he'd enjoyed hearing Miles describe his part in the play and share how excited he was to hand out invitations during the reception, Brent had missed the soft lilt of Zoe's voice beside him. He'd missed her happy tone, the way she sometimes nudged him with her elbow as he drove to make sure he was listening, how she would usually smile at him from the passenger seat and drum the dashboard with her hands in excitement over the holiday festivities.

His worries had eased later, though, when they'd arrived at the elementary school. Once they'd entered the auditorium and she'd caught a glimpse of the glittery props serving as Santa's workshop on the stage, the colorful Christmas lights strung artfully from the ceiling and the excited teachers and students adding their final touches to decorations to bring the holiday atmosphere to life, Zoe had perked up.

She'd jumped right in and helped him arrange a thick white rug and large red chair draped with evergreen garlands in the area reserved for Santa to greet children and pose for pictures during the reception. She'd even assisted one of the PTA members, who'd volunteered to take photographs, set up her equipment. When the first child had lined up, skipped over to Brent and hopped up onto his knee, rattling off a list of things to Santa that he wanted for Christmas, Zoe had enthusiastically assumed her role as Mrs. Claus.

Merriment had danced in her eyes throughout the past hour as she'd eagerly welcomed each child and helped them assume different poses as the camera clicked, the PTA volunteer taking pictures of each child who sat on Santa's knee, preserving the moment for their families. And many times, children who'd lined up to see Santa had requested to have a photo with Mrs. Claus and baby Holly, who was dressed in a red onesie with faux-white-fur cuffs and collar as well. Zoe had delighted in that, hugging each child close to her side as she'd cradled Holly and smiled wide.

Over the past hour, the long line of children had dwindled down, Amelia was the last child in line, and it was close to showtime. Miles and Emmett had stood nearby, handing out the Christmas party invitations to each child as they'd moved through the Santa line. They had given all out but a few of them, and they were sure to have a full house at tomorrow night's Christmas party. There were only a few minutes left before the curtain rose and the play began, and Brent found himself wishing his tour of duty as Santa wouldn't end.

Zoe had been right—he enjoyed being Santa. This Christmas season had been the best he'd experienced in years. And he had Zoe to thank for it.

"I'm sure," Zoe said, smiling down at Amelia, who still sat on his knee, "there are a few redheaded baby dolls outside in Santa's sleigh." She winked surreptitiously at Amelia's mother, who nodded. "I'll take a look in Santa's bag when we're on the way back to the North Pole tonight and make sure I set one to the side for you."

Amelia beamed with joy. "Thank you, Mrs. Claus! And thank you, Santa."

Brent laughed as she hugged his neck, hopped off his knee and rejoined her mother. "I hope you have a very merry Christmas, Amelia."

"Okay, Mr. and Mrs. Claus." Joanie, the PTA volunteer who had been taking the pictures, removed her camera from the tripod and started packing up. "Y'all have done more than your fair share of tonight's work, and the play is about to start. Why don't y'all grab a seat and get settled, and I'll pack everything up?"

"Sounds like a plan." Zoe held out her hand to Miles. "I'll take whatever invitations you have left, Miles, and will finish giving them out after the play."

Miles handed the few invitations he held to Zoe, straightened his elf hat and glanced at the stage nervously.

"I went over my lines in my head so I won't forget them and practiced a lot yesterday with Mr. Emmett. I hope I do good."

Brent stood, walked over to him and knelt, bringing himself to Miles's eye level. The eagerness in Miles's expression as he sought approval made Brent wish he could put his arms around him and protect them from any disappointments in life. "You don't have a thing to worry about," he said softly, edging Miles's chin up gently with a knuckle. "You're gonna be an awesome elf."

"Do you really think so? You think I'll be a good elf?"

"You've done a great job of it over these past few weeks at the Santa mailbox." Brent tilted his chin up a bit higher. "You've worked hard helping others and bringing them joy. I'm already proud of you." He glanced up at Zoe and smiled. "And I know Zoe feels the same way."

Something changed in Zoe's eyes—a fleeting glimpse of pain, maybe?—but she looked away, lowering her head and avoiding his gaze.

"Thank you, Mr. Brent!" Miles hurled himself into Brent's arms, rocking him back on his heels and dislodging his elf hat. "I'm going to do my best, I promise."

Heart overflowing, Brent hugged him back, smoothed one hand over his thick hair and replaced his elf hat. "I know you will. Just have fun—that's all that matters."

Before he could draw another breath, Miles had slipped out of his arms, run over to the stage and bounded up the steps to join his classmates and teachers behind the curtain.

Emmett laughed. "Boy, I wish I still had that kind of energy."

"Don't we all?" Joanie laughed and smiled at Emmett. "Thank you so much, Mr. Lee, for greeting our kids so warmly tonight and letting us have our Christmas party in your beautiful home. The kids have been so excited since we told them, and when I drove by your place yesterday, I could see the decorations are coming together beautifully." She clapped her hands together. "Christmas in a gorgeous Victorian house! We'll all remember this year's party for years to come."

A pleased smile lifted Emmett's wrinkled cheeks. "I wish I could take the credit, but the ones you should really be thanking are Zoe and Brent. They've put in countless hours over the past few days hauling decorations down from my attic, dusting off furniture, shining up the silver and stringing lights on the porch. And they've already brought over dozens of frosted cookies, twenty different bags of potato chips and countless candy bars, cakes and pies." He chuckled. "My house has been boisterous and fit to burst these past few days, and I couldn't be happier."

"Wait till we pack your place full of kids," Joanie teased. "You might think differently then."

Emmett laughed harder. "Oh, I'm looking forward to it. Been sprucing up Christmas stories in my head and getting ready to tell them. And I got Miles and these two to thank for the excitement." He gestured toward Brent and Zoe. "Now, how 'bout we find some seats? I'm ready to see our young Miles light up the stage."

The lights dimmed as they made their way toward the back of the auditorium. Brent chose the last row of empty seats, where there'd be ample room for Emmett to stretch his legs out and sit in a comfortable position while he enjoyed the play. After they settled in their seats, Brent opened his arms to Zoe, who sat beside him. "Wanna give your arms a break?"

Zoe glanced down at Holly and grinned. "I think I'll

take you up on that. She's light as a feather, but after an hour of holding her, I could use a bit of downtime."

After she transferred Holly into his arms, Brent settled back against the seat and laughed softly as Holly stared up at his beard, her tiny fingers latching onto his beard's long gray strands. "You little ones love to yank on a beard, don't you?" He kissed her forehead. "That's okay, baby girl. Yank all you want."

A holiday song emitted from the large speakers installed on both sides of the stage then the curtain rose, revealing five boys and five girls who were dressed as elves and all looked to be around the same age—Miles among them. He stood in the center of the stage, his fists propped on his hips and a wide smile on his face as he and the other elves began singing and dancing to the peppy holiday tune that played.

"He's doing great," Zoe whispered, her hands curling around the edge of her seat as she leaned forward and smiled.

Brent studied her profile, the way she nibbled on her lower lip, the slight blush on her cheeks and pride in her eyes. She was such a wonderful mother and selfless, caring individual. A truly magnificent woman.

Something stirred in his chest. An unfurling of sorts, an overwhelming surge of affection that expanded his heart and thrummed strongly in his middle. He reached out, took her hand in his and lifted it to his mouth, brushing a kiss across the delicate skin of her wrist. The touch of his mouth was brief and tender—barely there, really—but her pulse fluttered against his lips and her sweet scent, reminiscent of peppermint cookies, filled his senses, making his heart hammer against his ribs.

After a moment, he reluctantly released her hand, lifted

his head and met her eyes. The surprised longing in her dazed gaze stole his breath.

"Why did you do that?" she whispered, a hopeful expression crossing her face.

Brent hesitated. He hadn't intended to touch or kiss her, for that matter. But tonight, sitting beside her, holding Holly and watching Miles perform on stage felt... right. That haunting guilt he used to experience around Zoe and the heavy regret he'd carried for years had begun to fade. Something new and strong had taken its place, only making itself known in this moment.

Hope.

After the past few weeks of celebrating the holidays with her, doing good deeds for others and leaning on Zoe for support, he found himself hoping that God would bless him with an opportunity to start over. He was hoping for a future in which Zoe, Miles and Holly would be a part of his life every Christmas and every day from this moment forward.

He stared down at her, his mouth opening soundlessly, wanting to tell her that he was ready to let go of the past and embrace something new, wanting to hear her say she felt the same. But he was unable to bring himself to say the words.

Instead, he lowered his head again and leaned closer, speaking against the soft shell of her ear to be heard over the holiday music that swelled throughout the auditorium. "To thank you. I haven't enjoyed Christmas this much in years. Thank you for inviting me to be a part of this, Zoe."

He didn't know what he expected her to say, but he hadn't expected the polite, impersonal tone of her voice to cut him so deeply as she turned away, faced the stage and whispered, "You're welcome."

Chapter Ten

On several occasions prior to decorating, Brent had tried to envision how Emmett's house would look dressed up in the Christmas decor Emmett's late wife had carefully chosen for their Victorian home. But in all his imaginings, he hadn't come close to the opulent splendor of the Queen Anne–style Victorian home as it looked the night of the elementary school Christmas party.

"It's a dream." Brent, standing on the dormant front lawn in the crisp December night air, tipped his head back and took in the impressive sight, a smile curving his mouth. "An absolute dream."

"Amen." Emmett, who stood by his side, clapped a hand on his back and squeezed his shoulder. "You, Zoe and those PTA parents did a fine job decorating this beauty with Constance's decorations." He smiled broadly, beaming up at his home. "Constance and I had some gorgeous Christmases in this house over the years, but I've never seen it glow with so much joy before. She'd be prouder than ever of it, if she were standing here now, beholding it like we are."

"This was mostly Zoe's doing. She was the brains of the operation, and I was more or less the grunt." Brent chuckled. "The PTA parents and I simply followed orders as she gave them."

Emmett laughed with him. "Well, as particular and organized as that gal is, if someone let her, she could very well run the world and do a better job of it than most."

Still smiling, Brent admired the festively decorated house before him. Evergreen garlands, adorned with full bows, red berries and flocked pinecones, trailed along the banisters of the wraparound porch. Velvet ribbons wrapped around the columns supporting the house, lush wreaths had been hung over every window and bright white Christmas lights were strung strategically along the gabled roofs, porch railings and facade of the home, lending the entire structure a warm glow of holiday welcome.

The Christmas decorations he and Zoe had unboxed in Emmett's attic had been almost exactly the treasures Zoe had envisioned and so much more. Zoe had carefully planned every detail of how each decoration would be displayed outside.

But the interior of the house—Brent shook his head in awe at the thought—was even more impressive. Emmett's late wife had packed away a Christmas tree for almost every room of the house, and each room that would be utilized for the Christmas party had been graced with one decorated with a unique theme. One tree was decorated with angels, another with snowmen, a third with elves and Santa's reindeer, and yet another, an eight-foot-tall live tree set up in the foyer of the home, had been decorated in traditional shades of red and gold. Every fireplace mantel throughout the house had been graced with garlands, lights, glittering ornaments and bows, and even the bathrooms had been included in the holiday cheer, decorative swags and festive figurines positioned prominently among the light fixtures and beside the sinks.

In addition to decorating with zeal, Zoe had considered the age and interests of every child who would attend the party and had used various items from Emmett's attic as well as donations from the school's PTA to make the event an enjoyable occasion. Board games, video games and toys had been set up in one room; a Christmas tea set with Constance's collection of vintage dolls in another; and snacks, main dishes, a glass bowl of punch and goodie bags had been arranged on the large dining table that was covered in a white lace tablecloth. But the true highlight of the occasion was a cozy reading nook that Zoe had arranged in the sitting room by the fireplace, where Emmett would sit later that evening and share his Christmas stories with the children.

No detail had been too small or overlooked, and the final festive splendor of their four days of work had made every drop of sweat, every heavy breath and every sore muscle worth it.

"It's wonderful," Brent said. "Just like Zoe promised. What is it about a Victorian house decorated for Christmas that makes it so appealing?"

"It's not the house," Emmett said softly. "It's the season. Constance used to say she preferred having a romantic date with me at Christmas over Valentine's Day every year. There's no greater season for love than Christmas, she'd say. It's a time for love, joy, generosity and all the good a heart can hold. God's gifts, she used to say."

Brent nodded, then glanced over his shoulder at the quiet street behind them, straining to catch a glimpse of headlights approaching along the darkened road. Zoe should arrive any minute, and he couldn't wait for her to see the final product of their hard work sparkling brightly for the first time beneath the night sky.

His smile fell. He wished she would've taken him up on

his offer to pick up her, Miles and Holly and escort them to the party himself. But after finishing up last-minute decorations earlier that afternoon, Zoe had declined his offer and left Emmett's house an hour before dark to return to her cabin, feed Holly and get herself, Miles and Holly dressed for the party. She'd promised as she'd left that she would return with Holly and Miles a few minutes before guests were to arrive.

Sighing, Brent faced the house, the beautiful sight lifting his spirits again. She hadn't seen the house after dark yet. Not as it was now, completely decorated and ready to welcome children. Emmett's home was truly a sight to behold, and he looked forward to seeing the joy on her face when she did finally see the Victorian house at its best.

"Zoe's going to love it." Brent looked at Emmett and smiled. "Thank you for giving us this opportunity. I know the sight of your house alone, like it is, will be the highlight of Zoe's Christmas."

"Oh, I don't know about that." Emmett tilted his head, licked one fingertip, then lifted it in the air. "You feel that? That winter wind is shifting, and I think the cold front they've been predicting is gonna roll in earlier than expected." He grinned. "My nose is telling me we might get some snow soon. The first dusting of winter snow might even settle in before Christmas. And wouldn't that be a sight to behold?"

Brent glanced up at the night sky, the frigid air chilling his cheeks. "It would, but that'd be a long shot. We don't usually see the first flakes in our neck of the woods until at least a week after Christmas."

"Ah, but this is a season for special blessings, and God's in charge of those." Chuckling, Emmett squeezed his shoulder and headed toward the front porch. "Come on. There's one final touch we need to make to the decorations before our job is finished."

Brent followed Emmett inside and joined him at one of the large windows beside the front door of the house.

Emmett picked up one of two large candles that sat on a small table near the window and smiled. "This one's for you, Constance." He grabbed a book of matches that lay nearby, withdrew and struck a match, then lit the candle he held and placed it gently on the windowsill in the center of windowpane. "I still miss you every day."

Brent moved to speak, then hesitated, biting his lower lip. "Did you ever fall in love again?"

Emmett shook his head. "No. I never met another woman who could steal my heart like Constance did. It belonged to her the moment we met and has ever since."

"Do you think you could have, though?" Emmett met his eyes, and Brent looked away nervously before forcing himself to meet his gaze again. "If you did happen to meet the right woman. Do you think you could've fallen in love again?"

"I suppose I could have," Emmett said softly. "That is, if God saw fit to send me someone new."

"But…" Brent dragged his clammy palms over his jeans. "Do you think that it would've been possible for you to move on from Constance even if you loved someone new?"

Emmett held his gaze, the older man's eyes roving over Brent's face, peering past his expression, probing deep, as though he were trying to pick apart his thoughts. "Might this have something to do with Zoe? Have you fallen in love again, Brent?"

Gut churning, he lowered his head and studied the unlit candle on the table beside the window, remaining silent.

"I believe there are a lot of seasons in our lives," Emmett said. "And I also believe God has a purpose for each one." He smiled. "I was never blessed with a new season of love after Constance. But if God had sent a blessing like Zoe my way, I'd like to think I'd be able to warm up to the idea and not turn my back on her."

"Even though you promised your heart to Constance? You wouldn't have felt guilty about moving on and loving someone new?"

Frowning, Emmett shook his head. "Moving on is what Constance would've wanted me to do. She would've wanted me to fall in love again. To be happy again." His smile returned. "And I know that's what Kayla would want for you, too." Emmett looked away, his gaze drifting back to the lit candle he'd centered behind the large window. "There's room in our hearts to love more than one person, and moving on doesn't mean erasing the past. Loving someone else doesn't mean you have to forget Kayla or that you loved her any less." He fell silent for a few moments, then looked up and squeezed Brent's shoulder gently. "Let's get Kayla's candle in the window, shall we?"

Nodding, Brent followed Emmett's lead, picked up the second candle from the table and walked across the foyer to the window on the other side of the front door. He lit the candle and placed it on the windowsill, the flickering flame of the candle dancing before him, reflecting on the glass pane and stirring a deep ache within him. He reached out once more, looping his finger through the brass handle and nudging the candle a bit more to the left.

"Zoe's here," Emmett said beside him, pointing at the road outside where a white Jeep drew to a halt in front of the house.

Brent watched as the driver's side door opened and

Zoe got out, shut the door behind her and walked a few steps toward the house.

She stopped and stared, a broad smile spreading across her face as she tilted her head back, her excited gaze roving slowly over the decorated home. She wore a pink dress with a rich red bow around her waist, reminiscent of those they'd placed on the Christmas tree in the foyer. Her blond hair was down, spilling in long, shiny curls around her shoulders.

Breath catching, he leaned closer to the window. She couldn't possibly look more beautiful if she tried.

Her attention moved to the window, her gaze fixing on his, then lowering to his hand, her bright smile dimming.

Brent stared back at her over the flame that flickered between them, his hand still curved around the brass handle of the candle, standing in the present but clinging to the past, unable to let go—even as the future he wanted stood, waiting, right before him.

"This is the best party ever! I made reindeer antlers out of balloons, won third place at Christmas charades, helped build a gingerbread house..."

Zoe smoothed Miles's tousled, slightly sweaty hair from his forehead and smiled down at him as he rattled off the activities he'd enjoyed during the prior two hours.

And boy, had there been activities!

In addition to the experiences Miles had enjoyed so far, Zoe had set up several other fun stations throughout the rooms of Emmett's house that she hoped would offer entertainment to all children who attended the party. There was a Guess the Number station where glass jars of various sizes had been lined up on a table and filled with different Christmas candies such as gumdrops, candy canes, chocolate kisses and marshmallows. Each partygoer could write down his or her guess as to how many of each candy were in each jar, and the partygoer who guessed the closest to the actual amount would win a small door prize.

She'd set up another station in a corner area of the kitchen where a volunteer from the PTA had offered to paint stars, trees and other seasonal requests on children's cheeks and hands. Other moms who volunteered with the PTA had set up their own gathering on a cozy couch to take turns holding Holly, cooing, kissing and admiring her. At several additional stations, children and parents cut out snowflakes and decorated them with glitter, painted Christmas trees and strung freshly popped popcorn onto strings to make old-fashioned garlands for their Christmas trees at home.

But the most popular station of all was a story nook in the sitting room, where Emmett sat in a cozy chair by the warm fireplace as children and their parents gathered around, sipping hot cocoa and listening to his many stories of childhood Christmases in Hope Springs. Each story made the most unique details of the Victorian house all the more interesting as they were described through the lens of Emmett's nostalgia for past holiday seasons. After each story, parents and children toured the home, finding secret nooks and crannies, photos and objects that had been mentioned in Emmett's Christmas stories.

And the entire evening had lifted Emmett's spirits even more than Zoe had hoped. She'd caught a glimpse of pride in Emmett's eyes on several occasions as he'd noticed others lingering in the hallways or studying antiques on the mantel with avid interest and admiration.

Tonight's Christmas party had not only offered the children, parents and teachers an opportunity to celebrate the holiday in a fun, new way, but the exuberant children and family-friendly activities had also brought Emmett's home to life again. If the boisterous laughter coming from Emmett's direction all night was any indication, the holiday party had granted Emmett his wish: one more wonderful Christmas in the house he loved before he had to move on to a new phase in his life.

Even now, the excitement in Emmett's voice as he told a story in an adjacent room made all the hard work worth it. Zoe's heart felt fit to burst.

"...and I want to do the snowflakes and the face painting and go play freeze tag in the backyard," Miles was saying. "And I want to eat some more chips and drink some more punch and—"

"Hold up there a sec with the chips and drinks!" Zoe laughed, cupping Miles's flushed face with her palms. "I think you've had quite enough sugar already. If you eat anymore, you'll probably shoot through the roof and into space under your own steam."

"Then I guess we oughta take our turn in line with pinning the nose on Rudolph before he runs out of gas."

At the deep throb of Brent's voice, Zoe glanced up, his gorgeous smile and charismatic appeal warming her cheeks as they had all night even though she'd tried her best not to focus on him.

It had been tough keeping her distance, though. Tonight had been the first time she'd seen Brent fully shed his dour disposition and relax in the company of others. For the past two hours, he'd been all smiles, laughter and easy conversation and had worked hard to make sure every child felt included in the festivities and every parent and teacher felt welcome. And to top it off, he'd donned a dress shirt with his usual jeans and boots—one a dark forest green that deepened the rich brown in his eyes. The kindness in their depths made him more approachable.

Altogether, this was a side of Brent she had not yet experienced, and unfortunately, it made her love him all the more.

"It takes two people to play the Rudolph game, and Miles already has a partner," Brent said, flashing that dashing smile of his down at her. "So that leaves you and me." He held out his strong hand, palm up, in invitation for hers. "How about it? Be my partner?"

Zoe glanced across the room to where a cluster of kids and several adults had gathered in pairs, waiting for their turn to pin a red nose onto a large poster of Rudolph that was taped to the wall. One father and daughter were already playing—the father, blindfolded, stumbling and grasping blindly at air as his daughter shouted directions from her stance beside the Rudolph poster several feet away.

Zoe laughed. "Oh, no. That's an accident waiting to happen. I think I'll sit this one out—"

"Come on, Zoe!" Miles bounced up and down in front of her, his expression pleading. "Almost everyone's done it but us, and Mr. Brent can't play without a partner. I already have someone, but Mr. Brent doesn't have one, so he needs you to be his."

Zoe shook her head. "I'm sure Mr. Brent can find another partn—"

"Oh, please, Zoe," Miles begged. "There's a prize for whoever gets closest. A whole basket of peppermint cookies!"

Zoe laughed again. "Yeah, I know. We're the ones who spent hours baking them."

"Then that's all the more reason for you to take a shot

at winning them." Brent slipped his hand into hers, weaving his fingers between her own, and tugged. "Just one round—what do you say?"

"Oh, all right." Zoe ruffled Miles's hair one more time, then allowed Brent to lead her across the room.

She tried not to focus on his broad shoulders and lean length as he walked in front of her or dwell on the way his hand cradled hers, his callused fingers gentle against her own.

Good grief, being in close proximity with Brent was the last thing she needed. It'd been next to impossible to put distance between them though, considering every time she turned around, he seemed to be there smiling, laughing or engaging her in conversation. He'd even cradled Holly in his arms during one of Emmett's story sessions, slowly swaying from one booted foot to the other as Emmett told the story, smiling down at the infant in his arms and stirring all sorts of images in her mind as to how great a father he could be to Miles and Holly.

But none of that was to be, and she'd be better off letting go of that dream now.

After waiting in line with Brent for a few minutes, it was their turn.

"And our next participants are Zoe and Brent—our fantastic Christmas party hosts!" Joanie, the PTA member who'd taken pictures at the school play, had taken up the task of leading the Rudolph station. Smiling, she walked over and handed Brent a blindfold and red sticker in the shape of a nose. "One of you will be blindfolded and one will be a guide. I'll leave it to you to choose." With that, she returned to the Rudolph poster that hung on the wall and swept one arm in that direction. "When you're ready, spin your blindfolded partner around three times and give it your best shot."

"You ready?" Brent stepped in front of Zoe and smiled as he lifted the blindfold toward her eyes.

"Wait a minute. Why do I have to wear that? Why not you, and I do the guiding?"

Brent chuckled. "After being bossed around by you for the past three days with the decorations? I don't think so. It's my turn to supervise. Besides, these games were your idea, so it's only fair that you get to take part in at least one."

"Whatever." She closed her eyes and lifted her face. "Go on and get it over with."

"Yes, ma'am."

Zoe's lips twitched and she stifled a smile as Brent's warm hands placed the blindfold over her eyes and tied it at the back of her head, his fingers gently smoothing her hair safely away from the knot.

"Is that tied too tight?" His stubbled cheek brushed her temple as he spoke next to her ear. "Or just right?"

She cleared her throat, taking a moment to steel herself against his intoxicating presence. "It's fine, thank you."

"Okay, three spins and you're off." His big hands settled on her shoulders, then spun her around, twirling her in a full circle, then another and another, her stomach dipping with each turn as the supportive warmth of his presence greeted her each time she faced him.

Finally, the spinning stopped, and his hands left her shoulders. The floor dipped beneath her feet, and she smiled as she threw her arms out, seeking to steady herself amidst the chorus of laughter surrounding her.

"Go, Zoe!" Miles shouted. "Get it right on the bull's-eye and win the prize!"

Zoe laughed. "I'll do my best, but it's all going to depend on the quality of directions I'm given."

"You doubt my supervisory skills?" Brent's chest brushed her shoulder blades, the teasing note in his voice as he spoke near her ear again making her smile even wider. "Walk straight ahead, ma'am. Slow and easy."

She took one step forward, sweeping the toes of one foot across the floor in front of her and grasping empty air with her hands. "Are you sure I'm going in the right direction? I can't feel anything in front of me, much less a wall."

Brent's laughter sounded to the left, then front of her. "You're a ways off yet. Keep coming."

She took another step, then another, then—

"No! Not that way." Brent's voice sounded again to the left but this time farther off. "To your left. Follow the sound of my voice."

She nodded, trying her best not to picture him standing there waiting with a bright smile.

"Keep walking in the same direction you are now. Keep following the sound of my voice, and you'll be right where you need to be."

Oh, if he only had any idea what he was saying. How much she wanted to walk straight into his arms and into his life. But this was just a game, which would end all too soon.

Zoe tried to open her eyes behind the blindfold, her lashes catching on the soft cloth. "Am I almost there?"

"Yep. Just take two more steps, then stop."

She did as he suggested, stepping carefully.

"There you go," Brent said. "The poster's right in front of you."

She eased her right arm out, and her fingers, carefully

holding the sticker, guided the red nose toward what she hoped was the poster.

"A little lower," Brent called out. "A little more—that's it! Stick it!"

She did, pressing the sticker firmly onto the poster, and a chorus of cheers went up from the small crowd surrounding them.

"You did it, Zoe!" Miles shouted.

Zoe slipped off the blindfold and smiled as she looked at the poster. She had indeed done it. She'd stuck the nose in exactly the right spot, beating out all the other noses that had been stuck haphazardly to the poster.

"Can't get any closer that," Joanie said, laughing. "Folks, we officially have a winner!" She grabbed a large basket filled with peppermint cookies and placed it in Zoe's hands. "There are enough peppermint cookies in here to feed Santa's reindeer for a week."

Brent laughed. "Santa's reindeer are going to have to be pretty fast to gobble these up before we do."

"We're going to eat some tonight," Miles said, raising to his toes and craning his neck for a better peek in the basket. "The two in the back with the most frosting are mine." He looked up and smiled. "Are you coming home with us tonight, Mr. Brent? After the party? We can have cocoa and cookies with Zoe like we usually do."

Joanie's smile widened, her eyes sparkling with interest as they moved from Brent to Zoe, then back again.

Oh, boy. Zoe shook her head and clutched the basket close to her middle. Hope Springs's rumor mill would be in full force if she didn't nip this rumor in the bud soon. She'd have to have that talk with Brent sooner than she'd planned.

Zoe tightened her grip around the basket. "It's been a

long day, Miles, and Mr. Brent has worked hard on decorations the past few days. I don't think he'd want t—"

"I'd love to." Brent, smiling warmly down at Miles,
reached out and nudged the boy's chin up with a knuckle.

"No." Zoe looked up at Brent, meeting his eyes, pleading silently with him. "I don't think it's a good idea."

Brent's brow creased as he shook his head. "Why not?
Miles will be on a sugar high for quite some time after we
leave the party, and Holly will probably go right to sleep
once we get her back to the cabin, considering all the attention she's gotten tonight."

Zoe glanced over her shoulder where several of the
PTA moms were still gathered across the room. One of
them held Holly while the others looked on, smiling down
at her and murmuring sweet nothings. The moms had
doted on Holly all night, changed her diaper twice, fed
her a bottle of formula and were still taking turns holding her, babbling down at her and admiring her red hair.

Their attention and babysitting had been a huge help
for Zoe, who'd spent most of the night darting from one
side of the house to the other, helping make the party a
success, but she missed Holly already, and she'd been
looking forward to returning to the cabin with Miles and
Holly so that she could tuck them into bed and get some
much-needed rest.

"Why can't Mr. Brent come over?" Miles asked. "He
can help me put Holly in her crib, and we could tell her one
of the Christmas stories Mr. Emmett told us." He glanced
up at Brent, an eager expression appearing. "Can't we,
Mr. Brent? You'd like that, wouldn't you?"

Brent smiled and hugged Miles to his side briefly. "I
sure would, buddy."

Zoe blew out a heavy breath. "Miles, why don't you

check out the snowflake station for a few minutes while Mr. Brent and I talk in private?"

Miles frowned, confusion in his eyes as he studied each of them, but he complied, mumbling "Okay" and walking across the room toward the activity station.

Before she lost her nerve, Zoe headed for the door, asking Brent over her shoulder as she went, "Would you help me put this in the car, please?"

It was a silly request, but Brent followed her outside, down the front porch steps and across the lawn to her Jeep which was parked by the curb.

Outside, the night air had grown colder in the two hours since the party had started, and Zoe shivered in the wintry wind as she tugged her keys out of the small change purse hanging around her wrist. "I'm sorry, Brent. I didn't plan on having this conversation tonight, especially here. But this is too important to put off any longer." She opened the back door of the Jeep, set the basket of cookies on the seat, shut the door and faced Brent. "We can't do this anymore."

Brent stood there, staring down at her for a few moments. "We can't do what, Zoe?"

"Whatever this is." Face heating, she motioned between them. "Being neighbors, friends, whatever we are. You coming over so much is not in Miles's and Holly's best interests."

Brent frowned deeper, a wounded expression appearing. "What do you mean? We've had so much fun together these past weeks. I know I behaved like a jerk the first time I called you, but I thought I've made it up to him— and you. I apologized to Miles for my initial behavior quite some time ago. And I thought Miles and Holly enjoyed me coming around."

"They do."

"But you don't?"

"No," she said softly. "I love spending time with you—we all do—too much, actually…and that's the problem."

Brent closed his eyes, shook his head, then stepped closer, taking her hands in his. "This doesn't make sense to me. What is it you're trying to say?"

Zoe studied the way he cradled her hands in his, his thumbs brushing gently over her wrists. "Miles gave me his letter to Santa yesterday, before you picked us up for the Christmas play. Do you know what he asked for?"

Brent dipped his head, leaning closer. "No."

"He asked Santa to ask God if he, Holly and I could be a family." She lifted her head and met his gaze, trying to ignore the hot blush that snaked up her neck and suffused her face. "And he told me that he wanted to ask you if you would be his dad."

The sentiment had the effect Zoe expected.

Brent's hands loosened around hers, and he took a step back, his mouth parting in surprise.

"He enjoys spending time with you," she said. "So much so that he wants you around all the time. And so do I." Her throat tightened and it was difficult to speak. "I know you said we could only be friends, and I understand that. I've accepted it. I thought I could spend this time with you, get to know you and enjoy having you in my life without asking for more. But that's not enough for me." She tugged her hands free of his and looked down again, staring at her pink shoes instead of the pity she knew would probably be in his eyes. "I love you." She laughed softly. "It broke my heart when I first met you, seeing you in such pain over the loss of your family. I even snuck into your yard and left Prince with you three years ago, hoping he'd cheer you up. That's how long I've cared about you. Lately, though, spending all this time with you...my feelings have grown."

He drew in a sharp breath. "Zoe—"

"But it hurts to be around you, knowing you don't feel the same way about me. And I can't do that to Miles. I can't let you break his heart like you broke mine...even though I know you won't mean to." She stepped back and forced herself to meet his eyes, a pang of sympathy moving through her at the pain in his expression. "I've decided to adopt Holly and Miles, but that process is going to take some time, especially since we haven't located Holly's mother. In the meantime, I don't want to confuse either of them—or distract myself. My focus needs to be on building a family for the three of us, and that's why I think it's best to create some distance. It's best if Miles understands now that you're only a friend who will visit occasionally."

"And what if I feel differently?" The urgency in his voice surprised her. He moved closer, cradled her face in his hands and stared into her eyes intently. "What if I don't feel the same way I did a few weeks ago? What if I want something more?"

Zoe stilled, her heart pounding heavily in her chest. "Do you? Do you feel differently about me?"

She leaned closer and studied his mouth, willing it to move, hoping to hear him say what she'd hoped to hear for so long. Wishing he would say he loved her as much as she loved him and that he was ready to let Kayla go and begin a new life with her. But he remained silent and the defeated look of anguish in his expression told her nothing had changed...not really.

"This isn't your fault," she whispered.

She'd been foolish and unfair to spend all this time hoping for a different outcome. He'd told her himself, in the beginning, that there would be nothing more than friendship between them.

"I understand you're not ready to let Kayla go," she said. "It's just too painful to keep loving a man I know will never love me back. I need to move on. I hope you can understand that, too." Eyes burning, she blinked hard against the tears that threatened to fall and lifted to her tiptoes, kissing his stubbled cheek gently and whispering, "You're a good man, Brent. I wish you well."

Chapter Eleven

Two days later, Brent sat on the sofa by the fireplace in his living room, hunched over the cell phone in his hands, his fingers moving swiftly over the digital keyboard.

Good morning, Zoe. I'd like to check the mailbox one last time since it's Christmas Eve. Is that okay?

He bit his lip and stared down at the screen, waiting for the cell phone to chime and a new message to appear. One minute passed, then two, then five more before a response finally flashed across the screen.

Of course. Thank you.

Hands trembling, he scooted to the edge of the sofa and bent closer to the phone as he typed.

Would you, Miles and Holly like to ride with me?

He held his breath even as he shook his head. He knew what the answer would be. He shouldn't have asked, shouldn't have typed the question. But his fingers had moved faster than his good sense.

Since the school's Christmas party, he'd reluctantly

done as Zoe had asked. He'd given her, Miles and Holly space. He'd agreed to Zoe's request that she, Miles and Holly check the Santa mailbox on their own and he'd steered clear of the town square and had spent the time cleaning his cabin, splitting firewood and taking Prince for walks through the woods.

He'd been unable to take his mind off Zoe though and had gritted his teeth on multiple occasions, resisting the urge to drive over to her cabin and knock on the door just to say hi and see how she, Miles and Holly were doing. Zoe had asked for distance, and he found he couldn't deny any request she made to him, even if it hurt.

He deserved that though—the pain. He'd hurt Zoe more over the past few years than he'd realized, and for the past two nights, he'd tossed and turned fitfully in his bed, the expression on Zoe's face as she'd spoken to him outside of Emmett's house returning to his mind every time he'd closed his eyes. The anguish in her tone that night had been unmistakable, and the resigned look in her eyes as she'd walked away had left him feeling hollow and desperate.

You're a good man, Brent. I wish you well.

He rubbed his temples, his head throbbing as it had ever since he'd watched her walk away from him, unable to stop her. In that moment, standing there outside in the cold, watching her leave, he'd wanted so much to tell her that he loved her, to ask if they could start over—start fresh—with Miles and Holly, together as a family.

But the candle he'd lit only hours before, still flickering in the window of Emmett's house, had caught his eye. And he'd remembered the life he'd had with Kayla…and the promise he'd made.

He wanted to move on, but some small part of him, some tiny corner of his heart, still refused to let go.

A low whine sounded at his feet, and he glanced to his left where Prince lay sprawled out by the fireplace, his chin propped on his front paws and his sorrowful eyes blinking up at Brent.

Prince was yet another reminder of Zoe. To think, she'd cared so much about him years ago that she'd taken the initiative to bring the pup to him as a way of easing his pain. And all those years, he'd been so blinded by his grief that he hadn't opened his heart to her.

"I know, boy," Brent whispered. "You miss her, too, don't you?"

Prince whimpered and looked away, his big brown eyes focusing on the fireplace, growing heavy as he watched the flames flicker around the logs.

Brent shook his head. Zoe had done so much for him and had brought so much joy into his life and now he wasn't sure he'd have the opportunity to show her just how much she meant to him.

"Maybe she'll say yes," Brent said softly. "Maybe we'll get to go check the mailbox together one more time."

At the mention of the mailbox, Prince's ears perked up and he lifted his head from his paws, his tongue lolling out happily just as his cell phone chimed.

Brent looked down at the cell phone in his hands, and his shoulders sagged as he read the text.

No, thank you. I'm taking Miles and Holly to town to pick up the mailbox later this afternoon. We'll empty out any letters that get dropped in after you check it and then put it in storage until next Christmas.

Next Christmas. And a year without Zoe, Miles and Holly in between.

Heart aching, he hesitated, his thumbs lingering over the digital keypad, then he began typing again.

I could meet you there later, if you'd like? Help you load the mailbox in your Jeep and take you, Miles and Holly out for hot cocoa afterward?

He waited, his breath stalling in his lungs as he watched the next text come through.

Miles, Holly and I plan on attending Christmas Eve service at church tonight, and I need to hurry home and take care of a few things first. I can manage on my own.

Brent dropped the cell phone into his lap and dragged his hands over his face. The thick stubble lining his jaw rasped against his palms. He looked at Prince and summoned a half-hearted smile. "It's a no-go, boy."

Prince whimpered again, then plopped his muzzle back onto his paws.

Brent sighed. Well, he had a choice to make. Several, in fact. But this particular one was easier to make than he'd expected.

Brent stood, walked over to the front door, removed his jacket from the coat rack and shrugged it on. "Come on, boy. We might as well do something productive rather than sit here moping all morning. Let's go grab whatever letters are left in the mailbox and write a few more responses, huh?"

Prince rose slowly to his paws, stretched his legs, then

ambled toward Brent and followed him outside to the truck.

The drive into town was pleasant, and Brent took advantage of the relaxed silence to clear his mind, letting his gaze wander over the mountain ranges in the distance and studying the low, thick blanket of gray clouds in the sky. The cold front that had arrived two nights ago had settled in, driving down temperatures and adding an arctic chill to the wind.

When they arrived at Hope Springs's town square, Brent parked and tugged the collar of his jacket up higher around his neck before exiting the truck. He attached Prince's leash and led him to the mailbox.

"Sorry, boy," Brent said, rubbing Prince's furry head. "No antlers today."

It felt odd standing by the Santa mailbox without wearing his Santa suit, but there was no one to greet at the mailbox—no long lines of kids clamoring to mail their last Christmas wishes to the North Pole. When he'd first started participating in this project, Zoe had told him that the letters and visitors died down the closer it got to Christmas, and since it was Christmas Eve, the majority of the small crowds milling about Hope Springs's town square were either posing around the town's Christmas tree or hustling along the sidewalks, entering businesses or bakeries and leaving quickly with last-minute presents or fresh-baked goods for their Christmas feasts.

Brent glanced at his wristwatch, noting the hour, then patted Prince's head. "It's still early. The stores'll be open for several more hours, and it won't get dark for quite some time. Why don't we hang out for a while and see if anyone else shows up with a letter?"

And maybe they'd just happen to be here when Zoe

and Miles arrived. That way he'd at least get to see Zoe briefly once more before Christmas morning.

His stomach churned—regret, frustration and an eagerness he'd never felt before gnawing deep inside him.

An engine purred, and a white Jeep rounded the town's traffic circle, heading toward the town square. Brent's heart skipped a beat, and he craned his neck to the side, straining to catch a glimpse of the driver.

He smiled. "I think this might be her, Prince. Maybe she decided to check the mailbox earlier than she planned. We'll get to see her after—"

But the Jeep drove on, cruising past Brent and Prince. The driver, a man, honked his horn and waved at a group of people who were posing for a picture by the town's Christmas tree several feet away.

Sighing, Brent rubbed his temples again, the painful pounding in his head growing louder. He huddled deeper into the lining of his jacket and hugged Prince close to his side, keeping the pup warm as they braved the wintry wind for several more minutes with no sign of Zoe.

Soon the temperature dipped even more, chapping Brent's cheeks and making Prince shiver.

"Let's go home, buddy." Brent walked over to the mailbox, unlocked the back and grabbed the few letters that were left inside. He shut and locked the mailbox door, then led Prince back to the truck.

He drove back to his cabin slowly, mulling over what Zoe might've been doing at that very moment. Was she baking more cookies and frosting them with Miles? Holding and feeding Holly? Or maybe the three of them were huddled together on the couch in her living room, snuggled under a blanket, watching a holiday movie on TV as a warm fire roared in the fireplace.

Whatever they were doing at that moment, he wished more than anything that he was a part of it.

After arriving back at his cabin, Brent led Prince inside, stoked the fire and rubbed his back for several minutes, helping the pup get cozy. When Prince's eyes closed and he began snoring, Brent walked over to his writing desk and sat down. He shuffled through the handful of letters he'd retrieved from the mailbox, chose one at random, opened it, withdrew the letter and began reading.

Dear Santa,
I saw my daughter last week. She was with Zoe from Hummingbird Haven. The woman I was told could give children a good life.

Brent froze, his hands tightening around the paper in his hand.

My daughter looked healthy and happy. Her hair was just as red as the day she was born, and there was a little boy with her and a man. You might know the man—he was dressed like you—and he lives in the cabin where I left my daughter. I was worried sick after I left her there. I didn't realize I'd taken her to the wrong cabin until it was too late. I thank God every day for protecting Holly from my mistake. For allowing there to be a good man in that cabin who would ensure my daughter made her way into Zoe's arms.
I'm not from Hope Springs. I attend college fifty miles away and live in a dorm on campus. I'm a junior and only two years away from earning a degree. If I graduate, I'll be the first person in my

family to have a college education and a chance at a better life.

I love my daughter. But I also know that she deserves so much more than I can give her. I don't want her to have to wait or fight for a better life like me. I want her to have it now, from the very beginning, even if I can't be a part of it.

I planned to keep her and almost did, but I knew it wasn't the right choice for either of us. It was so much harder to give her up than I imagined. I tried every day after she was born, but the day I left her was the first day I could bring myself to go through with it. And I regretted leaving her every day since...until I saw her again in the town square last week.

She was safe in the arms of someone I know cares for her, surrounded by other children, warm and protected. Zoe, her son and the man from the cabin are giving my daughter a stronger sense of family right now than I can or probably ever could. I know my daughter will be safe and happy this Christmas. Though it breaks my heart that I can't be with her, it soothes my soul to know she's well, happy and loved, and that she's living the kind of life I've always dreamed of. I thank God every day for sending someone to love my daughter as much as I do.

I don't need any gifts under my tree—this is all I wanted.

Brent eased back in his chair, his eyes skimming the contents of the letter again.

I thank God every day for sending someone to love my daughter as much as I do. Slowly, he turned his head and looked across the room where his and Kayla's last Christmas tree had stood six years ago, decorated with care. He could still see Kayla standing beside it, her hands cradling her swollen belly, smiling wide.

She'd been so happy then. She'd been filled with so much joy she'd only seen a bright future for both of them, filled with a new life to love.

But if she had known what was to come, if she were standing here now, facing him after all they'd lost, knowing she and their daughter could never return to him, what would she say? What kind of life would she want for him now?

He pictured her, standing there now, smiling that beautiful smile of hers, wanting the best for him. Wanting him to move on and love again. To be happy with someone new. Wanting him to *be loved* by someone new.

I thank God every day for protecting Holly from my mistake. For allowing there to be a good man in that cabin who would ensure my daughter made her way into Zoe's arms.

What would've happened if Holly had not been left at his door? If Holly's mother had taken her to Zoe's cabin instead?

He would never have called Zoe. Miles wouldn't have found the letter he'd written to Kayla in the lone stocking that still hung from the mantel; he never would have snapped at the boy or had to visit Zoe and apologize; and he never would've agreed to participate in the Dear Santa project, dressing as Santa to do God's work, reading letters and responding with good deeds that had lifted his spirits and led him to ponder the good blessings God had brought into his life after so much pain. And he wouldn't be sitting here now, holding a letter from Holly's mother, one filled with words that untied a knot deep within his heart, releasing his last regrets, opening his heart completely, making room for someone new.

He stared straight ahead, still holding on to the memory of Kayla standing there, smiling back at him, recalling her promise that this would be the best Christmas ever.

I thank God every day for sending someone to love my daughter as much as I do.

Brent sat there for a few minutes more and read the letter again. Then he set the letter aside, picked up the lone page of stationery that still rested on the back of his desk and read the greeting.

My dearest Kayla...

He picked up a pen and wrote for a while, tears filling his eyes then receding as he finished writing, a smile returning to his face.

He gently folded the stationery in thirds, stood and walked across the room to the fireplace mantel. He removed the stocking from the mantel, slid the folded piece of stationery inside, then went to the attic, retrieved a small trunk from the corner and stowed the stocking in it.

After returning the small trunk to its corner in the attic, he returned to his desk and sat down, scanning the gray clouds hanging heavy in the sky. The stores were still open, there were several hours of daylight left and quite a few decorations at Emmett's house that had been left from the children's party that he could put to good use. Not to mention, if he asked nicely, a few volunteers from the PTA who'd doted on Holly the night of the school's Christmas party might be willing to pitch in if they knew it would brighten Holly's Christmas. With that kind of help, he just might be able to pull off one last Santa project for someone very special this Christmas.

Smile growing, he pulled out a clean piece of stationery and began to write.

It had been a good—and bad—thing that Zoe had brought home the basket of peppermint cookies she and Brent had won at the Christmas party. For the past two days, she'd found temporary comfort in those pink-frosted delights and washed them down with copious amounts of hot cocoa. But now, as she drove her Jeep toward Hope Springs's town square, she began to regret her sugar-laden emotional crutch.

"Can we get hot cocoa on the way back?" Miles, seated in the back seat beside Holly, clapped his hands in excitement. "One with extra whipped cream, marshmallows, sprinkles…"

Zoe's stomach roiled. She rubbed her belly with one hand and steered with the other, trying to keep the nausea at bay. "I don't think so, Miles. It's really cold out and will be dark soon. After we load up the Santa mailbox, I think we should head on back to the cabin and get a little rest before we leave for Christmas Eve service at church."

Miles perked up. "Oh, I can't wait to hear the choir sing. And when we get back, we can get ready for Santa." His smile fell as his eyes met hers in the rearview mirror, narrowing slightly. "But what snack are we going to put out for Santa when we get back from church tonight? There aren't any more cookies to leave out for him."

Yep. That was definitely a bit of judgment in his voice and, to be honest, she kind of deserved it.

"I told you I was sorry I ate all the cookies." She blushed. "I guess I've got a sweet tooth or something."

In actuality, it hadn't been a sweet tooth that had driven her to consume the peppermint cookies in a steady stream. It had been her breakup with Brent—though she really couldn't call it that, considering how they had only ever been just friends.

It was silly for her to wallow in self-pity like this during the holidays when there was so much to celebrate and so much joy to be had, but she just couldn't get Brent out of her mind…or heart. After all, the man had taken up a lot of space in both for years now. It should've come as no surprise that it would take quite some time before she could let go of him completely. Still, putting distance between them had been a lot more challenging than she'd envisioned.

Over the past two days, she'd reached for her cell phone on more than one occasion, wanting to call him and hear his voice. And it had been especially difficult to turn down his offer to help her load up the Santa mailbox this afternoon. But she'd declined, reminding herself to focus on Miles and Holly's happiness and that what she was doing was best for them both.

"I tell you what," she said, navigating her Jeep into a parking space by the town square. "After we take care of things here, we'll go home and I'll bake a fresh batch of peppermint cookies before we head to church tonight."

"And chocolate ones, too?" Miles piped from the back seat.

Smiling, Zoe nodded. "And chocolate ones, too."

It was colder than Zoe had anticipated, the blustery wind picking up speed and pushing hard against her back as she unloaded Holly's stroller from the back of the Jeep, removed Holly from her car seat and bundled her warmly under a blanket in the stroller.

Miles stood shivering nearby, his gloved hands shoved deep into his pockets as he hopped in place from one foot to the other. "I wish Mr. Brent were here. We could have stayed warm in the car while he loaded up the mailbox." He frowned. "I don't understand why he couldn't come with us."

Zoe pushed Holly's stroller onto the sidewalk, then led the way toward the mailbox. "Mr. Brent's a busy man with a life of his own," she told Miles over her shoulder. "We can't call him for help with every little thing."

"But this isn't a little thing. It's *our* thing. You know, the Santa thing? He always dresses as him and we always dress as elves when we check the mailbox."

Zoe sighed. "Yes, but this time's a bit different. It's Christmas Eve and everyone has mailed their letters by now, so all we're here to do is pack up and go home. In light of that, there was no need to bother Mr. Brent."

She stopped the stroller beside the Santa mailbox and glanced at Miles, nibbling on her lower lip as she studied his face. He looked disappointed, as she'd expected, but she hoped he'd miss Brent less as the days passed and that his discomfort wouldn't last long. On the other hand, she couldn't imagine hers going away any time soon.

"I guess not." Shrugging, Miles walked around to the back of the mailbox, opened the latch and felt around inside. "There's only one letter this time." He withdrew one thick envelope from the mailbox and held it out toward Zoe. "Guess this'll be the last one."

The heavy, disappointed tone in his voice made Zoe sigh. "For this year," she said softly. "We'll take a break and enjoy Christmas Eve at church tonight and celebrate Jesus's birth tomorrow, and then next year we'll get to start all over again."

Miles smiled at that. "And we'll get to dress up like elves again?"

Zoe laughed. "Of course! We need elves to manage the Santa mail."

"And Santa!" Miles hugged his arms to his chest and shivered. "Mr. Brent can be Santa again next year, can't he?"

"We'll see." Zoe tapped his chin as his teeth chattered, taking advantage of the distraction. "But for now, we need to get this mailbox loaded in the Jeep and start home before you turn into an ice cube. It's freezing out here!"

The mailbox didn't weigh much but it was a bit cumbersome, and it took several minutes for Zoe to navigate her way across the town square to the Jeep and load the mailbox into the back. The wind gusted as she unstrapped Holly from her stroller and buckled her into her car seat.

"Whew!" Zoe opened the door for Miles, holding it open against the strong wind. "Hop in and let's kick this mule! We need to get home and warm up."

Laughing, Miles did as she asked. After he was safely buckled in, she drove back up the mountain to her cabin. She unloaded the mailbox, put it in the storage building behind her cabin, then took Holly and Miles inside and built a fire in the fireplace.

Zoe, cradling Holly, sat on the couch, kicked off her boots, lifted her feet and wriggled her socked toes in the air near the fire. "Come on, Miles. Grab that throw from the back of the couch and come snuggle with us."

"And then we'll make the cookies?" At her nod, Miles grabbed the throw blanket from the back of the sofa, sat down beside her and spread the blanket over their legs.

Zoe looked down at Holly and smoothed the baby's red

hair off her forehead. "Can't beat warm toasty toes on a cold day, huh, Holly?"

Holly's blue eyes fixed on Zoe's mouth as she cooed up at her in response.

"Here," Miles said, tapping Zoe's arm. "You can't forget the last letter. It's Christmas Eve, so you have to read it now."

Zoe grinned. "Thank you for reminding me of my duty, sir."

She took the envelope from Miles, slid her finger under the flap, opened it, then withdrew the contents. Two letters, rather than one, had been folded and stuffed inside the envelope. She unfolded them both, but one of them caught her eye first.

Dear Santa,
I saw my daughter last week. She was with Zoe from
Hummingbird Haven. The woman I was told could
give children a good life.

Zoe froze, her hands tightening around the paper in her hand. She continued reading, her eyes welling with tears as she read each sentence twice.

"Zoe?" Miles, a concerned expression on his face, snuggled closer and looped his arm around hers. "Who's that one from?"

Zoe looked down at Holly, who rested comfortably on the crook of her elbow, the baby's eyes growing heavy from the warmth of the blanket and rhythmic crackle of the logs in the fire. "It's from Holly's mother."

Miles grew quiet for a moment, then asked, "What does she say?"

Zoe smiled as she finished reading, her heart swelling so much it felt fit to burst. "That she's glad Holly is with us."

Miles blinked up at her and smiled. "And that she can stay with us? We can be a family?"

Zoe nodded, her throat closing with emotion.

Miles clapped his hands, then leaned over and kissed Holly's cheek. "Did you hear that, Holly? Your mom said you can stay with us and we can be a family." He looked up at Zoe, his eyes bright. "That means your prayers worked, Zoe! God gave us Holly for Christmas."

Zoe cleared her throat. "Yes. He certainly did."

"But who's the other letter from?" Miles asked.

Blinking rapidly to clear her vision, Zoe set the first letter aside, picked up the second one and began reading.

Dear God,
You might think it odd that I put my letter to you in Santa's mailbox, but you and I have grown to know each other a lot better this year—thanks to Zoe!—and I know it's You who brings good into the world...not Santa.

Zoe's breath caught, her eyes scanning the letter down to the signature at the bottom. It was signed by Brent. She continued reading.

Zoe said it couldn't hurt to talk to you again, that it could only help. And it has. Praying to you during my walks in the woods behind my cabin over the past few weeks has helped lighten my burden. You've slowly lifted my spirits and brought hope into my life even when I questioned your love.
I've spent a lot of Christmases alone, nursing

memories from the past, thinking of what might've been and wishing I could go back. But not once, in all that time, did I ever look forward and consider what good things could be waiting for me in the future.

I never thought about setting my grief aside and helping others. I never considered dressing up as Santa and bringing a little extra cheer to children during the holidays. I never imagined I'd meet two orphans—one of whom You led to my door—who would make me long to be a father again. And I never expected to fall in love again.

But all of those things happened...and they happened for a reason.

Zoe swallowed hard, her lips trembling.

Emmett told me not too long ago that he believes there are seasons in life. That You send new ones when we need them and that You have a purpose for each one. This Christmas season, You've already given me the greatest gift of all: love.

You've given me a newfound joy for life, a desire to find and contribute to the good that's left in this world, and the will to start over and build a new future.

I'm so grateful this Christmas. I'm grateful for the highs and lows, the time I had with loved ones I've lost and the time I might have with the loved ones I've found, and most especially, I'm grateful for the hope that Christmas brings. Hope for salvation. For new life and new love.

I hope Zoe can understand how I feel and how

much I regret the time that has been lost between us. But I also hope she understands what I have to offer her now: my heart, every corner in its entirety, belongs to her from this day forward.

   My one Christmas wish this season is this, Lord: Please send Zoe to my door tonight so that we can praise you together this Christmas Eve. Please let her know how much I love her, Miles and Holly and that I want nothing more in life than to support and protect them for as long as I live. I'm ready to start over, and I hope Zoe is willing to join me.

With my greatest thanks,

Brent

"Zoe?" Miles shook her arm. "Why are you crying? Did it make you sad?"

Zoe dropped the letter and touched her cheek where a salty tear trailed from her eye and pooled in the corner of her mouth. "No," she whispered. "I—I'm crying because I'm so happy."

Miles tilted his head, reached out and wiped a tear from her other cheek. "Happy about what?"

Zoe smiled, laughter spilling from her lips. "I'm happy that we're both getting the present we really wanted this year."

Miles's brows rose. "Which one?"

Zoe kissed his cheek and hugged him tight. "One that's waiting for us right now. One we may even be able to take with us to the candlelight service at church later tonight." She released him, sat back and dragged her forearm across her wet cheeks. "Would you like to go see it?"

The concerned look in Miles's eyes melted away at the

exuberant tone of her voice, and he smiled. "Yes, ma'am. I'd like to get it now if we can."

Zoe lifted her feet again and wiggled her toes. "Then let's get our boots on and hop back in the Jeep."

It took a while to bundle back up, load Holly and Miles back into the Jeep and drive farther up the mountain to Brent's cabin. Night had fallen, making it difficult to see farther than the headlights that pooled across the road, but Zoe managed it, turning carefully onto the graveled driveway that led to Brent's cabin. As they rounded the curve and drew closer to his house, hot-pink lights sparkled just around the bend.

"It looks like a gingerbread house!" Miles shouted from the back seat excitedly. He shimmied in his seat, craning his neck around the passenger seat for a better view of Brent's cabin. "There are lights all over!"

And there were. Hot-pink Christmas lights had been strung carefully along the length of Brent's cabin. The pink bulbs outlined each window neatly, trailed along the porch rails, hung from the eaves of the roof and had been tacked in neat lines around the front door.

"It's gorgeous!" Zoe parked the truck, thrust open her door and hopped out, taking a moment to admire the sparkling pink splendor before her.

"Is this the present?" Miles asked as he unbuckled his seat belt. "Did Mr. Brent put the lights up special for us?"

"This may be part of it, but I think there's more." Zoe unstrapped Holly from her car seat and placed her in the stroller. "Let's find out, shall we?"

She helped Miles hop out of the Jeep and held his hand as they walked to the porch steps, then they carried Holly's stroller up the steps and knocked on the front door.

There was a clatter, something scraped across the

floor inside the cabin, then footsteps approached. The door opened.

"You're here." Brent stood in the open doorway, a string of pink lights looped around his muscular arms, Prince by his side and a bright smile on his handsome face.

Zoe's gaze clung to his, the warm affection in his rich brown eyes making her belly flutter. "Yes."

Brent glanced behind him, somewhat sheepishly. "It's not quite finished."

"What isn't finished?" Miles asked, tugging Brent's hand.

Brent knelt, kissed Holly's forehead, then brought his eyes level with Miles and winked. "Why don't you take Holly inside and find out?"

"Yes, sir." Miles pushed Holly's stroller inside, and moments later, his howl of joy emerged from the cabin and echoed across the cold landscape. "There's a big tree and pink stockings and lots of presents and—oh, come see, Zoe! Come see!"

Zoe bit her lip. "May I?"

Brent smiled and stepped back, sweeping one arm, still laden with pink lights, toward the interior of his cabin. "Please."

She walked across the threshold and stopped in the middle of the living room. There, in the corner, right in front of the window, stood the tallest, greenest Christmas tree she'd ever seen. Popcorn garlands and paper snowflakes, reminiscent of those children had made at the Christmas party, had been draped and hung along the full branches. Five pink Christmas stockings, one for her, Miles, Holly, Brent and Prince, hung from the mantel above a bright fire. Prince, busy tail wagging, pressed against Miles's legs and lapped at the boy's hands as he sifted through the gifts under the tree. Then the pup sat beside Holly's stroller, his tongue lolling happily.

"There's something for everyone!" Miles said. "Can I open one?"

Brent nodded. "Have at it. But only one, okay?" He slipped the string of lights off his arms, tossed them onto the couch and took Zoe's hand in his, his big palm engulfing hers as he led her toward the front door. "Zoe and I are gonna chat outside for a minute."

Zoe's smile widened as he led her down the front porch steps and out onto the front lawn. Her cheeks began to ache, but the happiness swelling inside her made it impossible to stop. "I can't believe you did all this, Brent!"

"Believe me, I had the best kind of help. You've done a lot of good for a lot of people this Christmas—including me." Facing her, Brent studied her face, then brushed his thumb across her lower lip. "It's good to see you happy."

Zoe smiled even wider. "I heard that you want to spend Christmas Eve with us at church. And that you love me."

"I do. On both accounts." Laughing, he stepped closer, his warm hands cupping her cheeks, blocking out the cold. "Very much so. I want to marry you and make a life with you. I want to adopt Holly and Miles, and I want us to be a family. Do you want that, too, Zoe?"

Zoe closed her eyes and rolled her lips together, shivering with joy. "Maybe," she teased. "But right now, I want to get another look at these lights you worked so hard putting up." She stepped back and spun away, tilting her head back and admiring the pink bulbs that twinkled against the log cabin. There were so many they lit up the dark like a pink bonfire. "It's quite a sight, you know? Although… a few bows wouldn't be too unwelcome. Maybe one on each window and one on the—"

Strong hands spun her around, and Brent's head dipped, his warm lips meeting hers. Her heart leapt with joy, her hands curling into his soft flannel shirt as she kissed him back.

After a few moments, she opened her eyes and smiled up at him. "I love you with all my heart, Brent Carson."

Tenderness shining in his eyes as they roved over her expression, he whispered, "Mercy."

Grinning wide, she reached up and tugged his head lower, kissing him again. His lips pressed warmly against hers, but something cold and delicate sprinkled across their cheeks, then melted on their lips. She drew back, snowflakes catching on her eyelashes as she glanced up at the sky.

"A white Christmas," she whispered, her heart over-flowing.

"The first of many." Smiling, Brent wrapped his arms around her and hugged her tight. "Merry Christmas, Zoe."

* * * * *